The Spider King's Daughter

CHIBUNDU ONUZO

faber and faber

First published in 2012
by Faber and Faber Limited
Bloomsbury House, 74–77 Great Russell Street,
London, WC1B 3DA

This paperback edition first published in 2013

Typeset by Faber and Faber Ltd
Printed and bound by CPI Group (UK) Ltd, Croydon, CR0 4YY

The right of Chibundu Onuzo to be identified as author
of this work has been asserted in accordance with Section 77
of the Copyright, Designs and Patents Act 1988

A CIP record for this book
is available from the British Library

ISBN 978-0-571-26891-7

FSC
www.fsc.org
MIX
Paper from
responsible sources
FSC® C101712

2 4 6 8 10 9 7 5 3 1

This first fruit I dedicate to my Father in heaven

Chapter 1

Let me tell you a story about a game called Frustration. A dog used to follow me around when I was ten. One day, my father had his driver run this dog over in plain view of the house. I watched from my window. The black car purring on the grit, the driver's hands shaking as he prepared himself for a second hit and my father, sitting in the back seat, watching.

The car reversed. Again his tyres rolled over my dog and then he sent for me.

I was calm until I reached him, his head bowed in the black funeral suit that he wore throughout my childhood, his arms folded.

'I'm so sorry. I know how much that dog meant to you. I don't know how this idiot didn't see it.'

I knew he was lying. He knew I knew and in that moment, I felt an anger fill me, so strong it would surely have killed one of us if I let it loose. Somehow, it was clear to me that this would be the wrong thing to do. I strolled over to the dog and prodded it with my foot. Blood had streaked its fur and it was whining in pain. My father studied my face, searching for the smallest hairline of a crack. I just stood there, looking at the animal.

Finally I said, 'Daddy, please can we run over my dog again?'

Both he and the driver were visibly shocked. My father nodded. The driver shook his head, his knuckle bones popping out of his dark skin.

'Do as she says.'

'Aim for the head,' I said, leaning against the car and taking a perverse pleasure in the driver's shrinking away. I turned and walked towards the house in that stroll that children have on the first day of their summer holidays. I called over my shoulder almost as an afterthought, 'Daddy, please make sure he hits the head this time.'

Abikẹ: 1
Mr Johnson: 0

Every morning I wake up and know exactly what I have to do.

1 Bathe.
2 Make sure Jọkẹ does the same.
3 Eat breakfast.
4 Make sure Jọkẹ does the same.
5 Ditto my mother.
6 Take Jọkẹ to school.
7 Leave school for work.
8 Make sure Jọkẹ never does the same.

It has been my morning routine for about two years. Lately,

it has become more difficult to make number 5 happen. She cries when I ask her to eat. I have his voice, Jọkẹ tells me, so my mother's salty tears drip on to the slice of bread meant for breakfast. This morning when we left, she was still in her nightie with her hair scattered from sleep. There was a time she would have hated anyone to see her looking like this. Now she is like a tree in the dry season. Every day a piece of her old self falls off.

'Bye, Mummy.'

'Have a good day at school, both of you.'

I have told her that I don't go any more but sometimes she forgets. Once I shut the door, Jọkẹ came to life.

'Did you know Mrs Alabi had a baby? The one that lives there,' she said, pointing at a peeling door. 'It was a boy and she is very happy because finally her in-laws will leave her alone.'

'Jọkẹ, I've told you to stop listening to gossip.'

'It's not gossip if Funmi told me.'

'Who is Funmi?'

'Don't you remember Mr Alabi's daughters, Funmi, Fẹmi and Funkẹ? They came to the house when we moved. You didn't like them. You said they wore too much make-up. It's only Fẹmi that wears too much. The others are OK.'

We were by the main road preparing to cross. A few feet away, there was a footbridge. We had not taken it since the first day I walked Jọkẹ to school and found my pocket empty on the other side. A red Toyota passed, then a Benz, then a small break. I gripped Jọkẹ's hand as we dashed across.

'Don't talk to those girls,' I said once our feet touched the pavement.

'Why not?'

'Because I said so and I've seen one of them smoking.'

'Which one?'

'Her name started with F.'

'All their names start with F.'

'I know.'

'Why won't you tell me? I won't tell because last time you told me something and told me not to tell—'

As she talked, I watched Wednesday, a regular hawker on this route, chase after a black jeep with his sales rack clutched to his chest, his muscular legs pounding down the road. The driver was teasing him. Slowing down and then speeding up, moving towards the highway with Wednesday's money. For a moment, it seemed like Wednesday would make it. The moment passed. Slowing down into a jog and then an amble, he continued walking in the direction of the vehicle, unwilling to believe that the owner of such a fancy car would steal. As the jeep sped on to the highway, naira notes, like crisp manna, floated to the ground.

Bastard.

'Are you listening to me?'

'Yes.'

'Then what's your answer?'

'To what?'

✳ ✳ ✳

A man in a yellowing starched shirt shoved past, nearly pushing us into the road.

'Look, Jǫkẹ, I have to watch the pavement. This place can be dangerous.'

'Fine! Don't listen to me. I'm going to Obinna's party.'

'Who is Obinna?'

'I just told you!'

'Well, whoever Obinna is, you're not going to his party.'

When had she become old enough for parties? I had taken her to the market to buy her first bra and sometimes I woke to find red spots on her side of the bed. Still she was only fourteen, barely a teenager.

'Whatever. I don't like Obinna anyway. He has too many pimples.'

I took her hand again and was grateful when she did not pull away. Too soon we were at the gates of her school. She drifted forward, looking for her friends.

'Have fun at work.'

She said this every day though I had never explained to her what I did. Trader was the vague description I had given to my job and she had never probed.

'Have a good day at school. Make sure you wait for Miss Obong.' I had arranged for Jǫkẹ to walk home with her English teacher who lived near our block.

'Do I have to? Everyone goes home by themselves. I look

5

like a baby.'

'You have to.'

'I'm stopping once I turn fifteen. Deọla!'

She shouted and was gone, running through the gates.

Chapter 2

I don't usually buy things sold on the road. A hawker I met today made me break my rule. Our eyes caught in traffic and that was all it took for this boy selling cheap ice cream to start approaching my car. I turned my head but he continued to advance. A gap opened in traffic. My driver crawled across the space.

'Drive on.'

'Don't you wan buy something?'

'Drive on.'

My driver sped up. The hawker gave chase. Traffic eased up and we found ourselves skimming along the road. In the side mirror, I could see a figure running after us. Another fifty metres and the figure was still there, although smaller.

'Slow down.'

'Eh.'

'I said slow down.'

This hawker was a fast runner. There were only ten metres between us.

'Speed up.'

'Eh.'

'Speed up!'

The car jerked ahead. Now the idiot was going too fast. I could see the hawker disappearing behind us.

'Slow down! Slow down!'

My driver pressed his foot on the brake bringing the car to a sharp standstill. I grabbed the armrest but the momentum pitched me to my knees.

'Aunty, sorry o.'

'Can't you follow the simplest instructions?'

As I struggled back into my seat, my elbow pressed a button and the window slid down.

'But—'

'But what? Don't you listen? I didn't tell you to stop.'

'I no understand.'

'Idiot! I said slow down.'

I turned to find the hawker beside my car. He was very good-looking. Dark and chiselled like something out of a magazine. I glanced at what he was selling. Sugary milk, frozen and wrapped in plastic for distribution to the masses.

'May I have one, please?'

'What flavour?'

'Vanilla.'

'One hundred naira.'

I stuck a two-hundred-naira note out of the window and waited. You never pay a hawker until you have what you're buying firmly in your hand. I was given my change first, then my ice cream.

'Thank you.'

When he left, traffic had descended again, leaving every vehicle pressed against another. Once I was certain he was gone, I flung the plastic thing out of the window.

'Tomorrow, take this way home.'

There was a time I wanted to be a lawyer, though of a different kind to my father. He was a bad speaker, rarely went to court and had a squint from reading the small print of contracts. It was his colleagues who inspired. Sometimes they visited our house still in their black gowns, coming straight from a case I had read about in that morning's newspaper.

Law was not to be. Instead, I am a hawker now, a mobile shop, an auto convenience store. I have grown used to the work. There are days when the rain is so heavy that the water rises to my knees. Other times, peoples' tyres squash my toes and often people call me and then refuse to buy. I have learnt to appreciate the few customers who treat me like a human being.

There was a girl I sold ice cream to today. She was sitting in the owner's corner of a jeep although she was too young to have bought the car. Her small body leant against the door leaving most of the back seat empty. While I was observing her, she looked up. Briefly our gazes held and before she could look down and dismiss me, I strode towards her with my sack of ice cream. When I was a few feet away, traffic mysteriously disappeared. The jeep zoomed ahead.

I gave chase. Half-heartedly at first but when I saw the car slow down, I picked up speed. Ten metres from the jeep, it sped up again. I kept running. The car was beginning to diminish and so was my anger. Then the car slowed down. Something cracked inside me and all I wanted was to spit in the face of the girl in that back seat. Stringy, phlegmy, spit that would run down her shocked face. Once I was a few feet away, I knew saliva would be the last thing coming out of my mouth.

I heard shouting. It was coming from the jeep. I moved closer. From the back seat, the girl clearly said, 'I told you to slow down!' Suddenly everything was all right.

'May I have one, please?'

'What flavour?'

'Vanilla.'

'One hundred naira.'

I looked at her face while she was bringing out her wallet. Her skin was so smooth I wanted to slide my finger along it. She passed me a two-hundred-naira note with a smile that showed her perfect, white teeth. It would have been so easy to sprint off with her money. I gave her the change before placing the ice cream in her palm. Someone else would have to show her that the world was not filled with honest hawkers and unicorns.

'Thank you,' she said. Words I don't hear often. I nodded and walked back to the side of the road.

Chapter 3

'Funkẹ, which university are you going to?'

'My mum thinks I should choose Brown but I think it's too expensive. The tuition fees alone are forty thousand dollars. What about you, Chisom?'

'I think Duke. Their fees are even higher.' The whole class could hear the triumph in her voice.

'So, Abikẹ,' Funkẹ said, turning to me, 'have you decided where you're going?'

'Yale.'

The good thing about applying from Nigeria was that most of the process could be done by someone else. My father had paid a PhD holder to fill out my forms and sit the SATs for me. I had taken the exams under a different name and been pleased to see that my score would have been adequate.

'Wow. So, Abikẹ, how much are Yale's fees?'

'It doesn't matter, Chisom. The cost makes no difference to my dad.'

Forest House was filled with people like these girls: a little money, a lot of noise.

***

'Settle down, class, settle down.' Mr Akingbọla bustled in, his trousers gripping his buttocks. 'I said, settle down.'

Someone at the back shouted, 'Bum-master in the building.'

'Who was that?'

He turned to face us with his large nostrils flaring. 'I said, who was that?' He slapped the teacher's desk. 'Don't let meh hask hagain.'

When Mr Akingbọla was agitated, he spread his aitches freely. This always made the girls titter and the boys copy their fathers' deep laughs.

'Hexcuse meh, sir, have you travelled before?'

'How can he? He's too endowed for the plane seat.'

Again another wave of laughter swept through the room.

'Silence. Can you talk to your fathers like that?' He was fast descending into his trademark rant. We were spoilt, we were useless, we would never amount to much.

'Even if your parents are successful, you—'

Already, half the lesson was gone. A paper plane flew through the air and landed on his desk. This was getting ridiculous.

'Listen to Mr Akingbọla.'

I needed only one person to hear me.

'Listen to Abikẹ.'

'It's true.'

'Some respect, please.'

'Yeah.'

The class fell quiet.

'You will not succeed.' Mr Akingbola's voice rang out, our sudden silence reproaching him. He shuffled his papers, arranging and re-arranging until he was calm.

'Today, we are going to continue our lesson on titration. When we want to find out the acid concentration of a substance this process can be used. What other processes can it be used for? Chike.'

Chike answered and Mr Akingbola droned on, the questions that followed every statement always managing to miss me. I felt no need to display my knowledge. On previous occasions, when he had put me on the spot, the class was allowed to become uncontrollable. He learnt fast.

'Next week,' he said in closing, 'we are going to conduct a practical experiment on acid-base titration. Make sure you . . .'

I wonder if the hawker will be on the road today.

The Datsun stopped abruptly, narrowly missing my legs.

'Clear from there,' the driver said, banging on his horn.

'Are you mad? You no dey see road?'

'My friend, comot or I go jam you.'

'You dey craze? Oya jam me.'

'Comot.'

'I said jam me today.'

The man swerved into the next lane.

'Idiot.'

'Your mama,' I spread the five fingers of my right hand and spat.

Fire for fire: that is the only way to survive on the road.

When I first started I used to mind my manners. Yes please, no thank you, like my mother taught me, but those manners were for a boy who was meant to go to university and work in a law firm. She never told me what to do if a customer sprinted away with my money. She never gave me advice on how to handle the touts that came here sometimes asking for 'tax'. I had dealt with one that morning, a slim, feral-looking man.

'Trading levy,' he had said.

'I don pay your people already.'

'Nah lie.'

'I tell you I don pay. No harass me. They know me in this area.'

'Who are you?'

'You don't know me?'

He was clearly a newcomer unattached to the main body of touts or he would have called my bluff. Instead he spat and moved on to the next hawker.

'Trading levy.'

I looked round and saw that there were only a few of us left on the road. Traffic had eased which meant that it was time for our break. To save money, I rarely bought lunch outside but I liked to sit with the boys while they ate.

'Runner G,' someone said, announcing my presence to the group. They raised their heads from plates piled with rice and red stew, the cubes of meat almost invisible in the mounds. I slapped some palms and rubbed a few backs before joining the circle of hawkers.

The recharge card men are the undisputed leaders of our group. Their branded jerseys set them apart: yellow for MTN, lime green for GLO, red for VMOBILE. Next come those who sell the unusual: framed photographs of past presidents, pots, bed sheets, crockery. Then the food sellers of which there is a hierarchy: ice-cream sellers with bicycles, ice-cream sellers with sacks, foreign sweets, foreign fruits and right at the bottom of the list, anything local: boiled peanuts, scraped oranges, plantain chips. These local things were mostly for women, though sometimes a man who had fallen on hard times could find himself with a tray of groundnuts balanced on his head.

'So, Runner G, wetin you go chop?'

Already the owner of the *buka* was lumbering towards me, her large feet spreading dust with every step.

'Aunty, I no want chop today. Thank you.'

'Why now?'

'I'm not hungry.'

'You sure you no go eat?'

'I'm sure.'

She patted my head, depositing something slick on to my hair. 'Just manage this one.'

From a secret compartment in her bra, she drew out a clear plastic bag, unknotted it and slid a piece of fried meat into my hand.

'Thank you.'

She nodded before trundling off to another group.

'Abeg no sit here if you don finish eating.' Her voice was

15

harsh again, the Mama Put we all knew.

When I turned, the boys had smirks on their faces. 'Runner G, it be like say that woman want marry you.'

'Well, I have no marriage plans at the moment.'

'No be so I hear o,' one of the recharge card men said, his voice hoarse with mirth and cigarettes. 'This woman get serious plans for you.'

'Abi o? You are a young man. You still get bedroom power,' a fruit seller said, gesturing and leering at the same time.

I stood. 'I'd better be going. I have work.'

A chorus of jeering and cajoling rose from the group. 'Ah ah, oh boy no vex.'

'We just dey play.'

'You sef, allow now,' a fellow ice-cream seller said, pulling me back on to my chair. I let myself be dragged down. Not long after the conversation continued.

'You watch match on Saturday?'

'Yes o. Arsenal mess up.'

'No be so.'

'Nah so. Arsenal play rubbish. They no get good defence.'

'No talk nonsense. Arsenal get good defence. The referee just dey cheat.'

'Abeg leave football. You hear say they catch one senator with fifty million naira in his car?'

'That one nah old news.'

'No be old news. Nah last week it happen.'

'Another one don happen this week. Yesterday, they catch the man's wife with hundred million.'

'Just one family dey eat all that money?'

'Nah so I hear o.'

Chapter 4

What would Forest House people say if they saw us? Not that I care. In fact I wish one of them would drive past on a day I manage to keep the hawker for a few minutes after he has given me my change. I imagine their eyes leaving their business to follow us as he walks beside my jeep. The thought makes me smile.

I should be sensible and start taking another route but my magpie tendencies won't let me. The other day, as six ice-cream sellers flocked to my window, I was pleased to see that I could pick out my hawker easily. He stood almost a head taller than the rest and he had a shine the others lacked. He still refuses to ask for my name. If I were a hawker, I would kill to know a girl with a car like mine.

There is one thing I am uncomfortable with. He is friends with a beggar who is missing an arm and possibly a portion of his senses. This man tried to intimidate me by holding his oozing stump over my window and leering into the backseat. On one side I had my hawker; on the other was this creature. Of course I had to give him money. A whole five-hundred-naira note and all he could say was thank you. Maybe I can befriend a hawker but surely not one who speaks to beggars.

I met Mr T about a year ago, when I was still hawking sweets. We were both chasing after the same car and surprisingly he was faster. A full five seconds before me, his pus-filled stump was hovering over the polished window of the Benz.

On one side, I held up my rack and my customer pointed at a pack of Mentos. On the other, Mr T brought his stump closer to the transparent glass and his benefactress shrank and scrabbled for her purse. Out of one window fluttered a crisp two-hundred-naira note. Out of the other sank a dirty fifty. We were both tired from our dash and we ended up sitting next to each other on the side of the road.

'Would you like some mints?'

I offered the pack by reflex, immediately wanting to withdraw when I remembered how little I had sold. My father taught us to always act like waiters, or hosts as he preferred to say. He was an effacing man, always scanning a room looking for someone to serve. Offer your seat, offer a drink, offer your mints. It was easy to play the host when you were rich. I hoped the beggar would decline.

He took the pack, unwound the foil and placed a mint in his mouth. His jaws crushed this first white disk, then the next and the next until all that was left was the wrapping.

'How much?'

'It's a gift.'

'There's no free thing in Lagos. How much?'

'It's OK.'

'If that is so then follow me.'

I watched him walk away. The distance between us grew as pride and other things filled my head. You know you've fallen when you are a hawker that is friends with beggars.

The space widened.

If your old friends could see you.

It was about ten metres now.

If only he wasn't dead.

At this sickening note of self-pity, I propelled myself forward.

Under a nearby bridge was a pile of cardboard strips and scrawled above this heap was a sign that said: SIT HERE AND CARRY MY CURSE. Mr T took me there and asked that I sit. I bent my knees in compliance, read the message and promptly stood.

'I brought you here to pay you with something more precious than naira. Many have wanted to know what I am about to tell you. One man from America even asked for an interview. He came with a tape recorder and notebook. I refused him. You will be the first person to hear my story in the past twenty years.'

I knew that when you had fallen, the memories that charted your decline became invaluable. Yet, I did not want the story. It was too important to be exchanged for a pack of mints but it was worthless to me. Before I could say no, he had begun.

✳ ✳ ✳

'I haven't always lived like this and I used to be quite handsome. Or so my wife told me. You smile. Because you think I was incapable of being a husband?'

His stump waved my apology away.

'You are right, perhaps I was. She was never the same after I married her. I offered all the things eighties Nigeria promised, a good job, servants, two cars. We both failed and I ended up in Oilet Grand Insurance. Do you know it?'

I shook my head.

'It was a horrible place. All day I read claims that I knew I would deny. Seven years into what I thought would be the rest of my life, I was fired. No pension. No reference. After that, things started disappearing. First my wife, then the car, then the gateman, then finally the house. Still, when my daughter and I moved here, I was hopeful.'

The cardboard pile did not look big enough for two people. Perhaps the daughter had moved out and built her own cardboard house.

'She started to lose weight a few weeks after we moved here. Her skin became stretched like the pastry of a meat pie, a meatless meat pie. With our money almost gone, I had two options: begging or armed robbery.'

'You could have become a hawker.'

'It was not so easy in those days. The soldiers could come at any time and lock you up for illegal trading. I used to leave her here and work on a nearby street. I soon discovered that poverty was not enough to be successful.

'"You are lucky to have been born like that," I said one day to a beggar who had no left leg. He smiled with teeth that were bloody from chewing kola. "Oh, this one no be luck," he said patting his stump. "I still dey pay for it." God forbid! God forbid bad thing. Then her skin stretched tighter and her belly began to protrude. I went back. He gave me an address. I went there and—'

'Were you awake?'

'Of course I wasn't awake! What type of stupid question is that? You think it hurt less because I was unconscious?'

'Calm down, please.'

'I am calm!' He banged the cardboard, his head jerking up and down. I stood, eager to distance myself from this beggar who was attracting stares. 'Come back. I am calm now. You can come back. She died two weeks later because I was too foolish to remember that you can't beg while your stump is healing, you can't think for the pain, you can't feed your two-year-old daughter.'

I stood there unable to find words that would blend sympathy into my suspicions. Where were his parents? His relatives? His friends? And how had he slid into poverty so easily? Even in Lagos, the white collar was not so loose that one could be an insurance man on Monday and a beggar by Friday.

In our case, there had been clear signs. The domestic staff were the first to go. Then our garage emptied, then the flat-screen TV was sold, leaving a square patch lighter than the rest of the wall. Yet, it was only when the landlord came to our house with policemen that I realised that this phase of our lives was not temporary.

Still we didn't become beggars after we left Maryland. No relatives came to our rescue – my mother is estranged from her family and my father's relatives are too poor – but his friends gave generously in the months following his death. Even if there were no family members, did this beggar have no friends that could have tided him over till he found another job? And that he would have found another job, if he had really worked in an insurance company, was almost certain.

'The prophet promised that one day the opportunity for revenge would arise,' he said.

'Pardon?'

'So what is your name?'

'They call me Runner G on the road. What is yours?'

'They used to call me Mr T in my office.'

Chapter 5

'Is it possible to make a car break down on purpose?' I asked Hassan as I handed him the hawker's ice cream.

'Eh?'

Milky saliva flew through a gap in his teeth and landed on the dashboard.

'Don't say eh? Say pardon me?'

'Pah doon mi?' he repeated, his inflections twisting the words into the vernacular.

'No, not like that. Say after me: Paaaar-duuuuuhn-meee?'

'Paaaaaah-dooooooooooo-miiiii?'

It was hopeless.

'Is it possible to break down a car on purpose?'

'Pahdoomi? I get am correct?'

'You only say "pardon me" when you did not hear what the other person said.'

'Mo pah ḍọ.'

'Pardon?'

'If "pahdoomi" means I no hear you, then "mo pah ḍọ" means I have heard.'

'Just answer my question. Is it or is it not possible?'

'Aunty, if you press your foot down and push the—'

'So you know how to do it.'

He nodded.

'Tomorrow I want you to break down the car at the place where we see the hawker.'

'Aunty, no. I cannot do such a thing.'

'No?'

'I'm sorry. Your daddy no go like it.'

'My father has nothing to do with this, Hassan. You are my driver and you will make this car break down tomorrow or you will not have a job by the end of tomorrow.'

'Yes, ma.'

✳ ✳ ✳

'Start. We're getting close.'

Hassan looked at me through the rear-view mirror. 'I no believe I dey do this to your father's car because of a hawker.'

He wasn't just a hawker. He was a hawker I was considering adding to my collection of friends. I was tired of people who went to Forest House, or schools just like it.

Hassan slammed his foot down and the car made a whirring noise.

'Hurry before we pass the place.'

If after spending an hour with him, I discovered that beneath the good English he had the grasping manners and mindset of a street hawker, I would drive off and never take this route again.

This time, the sound Hassan made was doubled.

'Quick.'

A third time and the car slowed down. Smoke began to stream out of the bonnet.

'Hassan, can't you see the smoke?'

'Aunty, stop making noise. No be you who want car break down?'

Smoke continued to pour out but I was silent until the car came to a halt. When I flung the door open, the unexpected noise made him cower to the steering.

'Remember, wait an hour before you come back with a mechanic.'

'Why I must bring mechanic?'

'So it will look like the car actually broke down.'

I climbed out and made a visor with my hand. Cars drove past without bothering to stop. Passers-by did the same. I could see my hawker walking towards us with his sack of ice cream.

'What happened?' he asked.

'I don't know.'

I turned to Hassan. 'What happened?'

'You know—'

I gave him a look that sent him sprinting to the car front. When he opened the top, a cloud enveloped his head. By the time the fumes had subsided, my hawker was beside me.

'Maybe you should go and get a mechanic, Hassan.'

'What about you?'

'I'll stay here with the car.'

'Your daddy no go like it.'

'I'll be fine.'

'I'm not sure o, Aunty.'

26

'Hassan,' I said softly, because my hawker was there.
'Yes, ma.'
He locked the car and left.

Some of the girls on my road can be very forward. Like everyone who sells here, the road has made them brasher and louder. They spit with the boys, they argue with the boys, sometimes they even fight with the boys, scratching and biting until someone comes to drag them away. Yet, they never let us forget that they are girls. Their tops plunge low; buttons remain undone, cheap perfume clings to them. Not all are like this, but the ones I wish to speak to will not speak to me. They look down when I say hello, hiding their smiles behind their fingers until I am gone. When they do speak, I am sad to hear the broken words they call English.

Still, whether brash or shy, all the girls on my road have a grace to their movements that I have seen nowhere else. In my old school, many of the girls walked with their eyes sweeping the floor. They were always being judged either for their bra size or their fashion sense and they learnt to look down. On the road, none of the girls care who is watching, or if they care, it is because they want to give the watcher a good show. Not only do they glide gracefully with burdens on their heads, they bend to pick money that has been flung at them; dash across roads with cars zooming by and the most daredevil do all this with a child strapped to their back.

It was while I was watching a woman pass change to a conductor that the rich girl's jeep drove past with smoke streaming from its bonnet. I watched it come to a halt and wondered if I should go and see what was wrong. The traffic rush would not start for at least another twenty minutes. By the time I reached her, the driver was peering into the car, his white shirt in danger from engine oil, his watch glinting in the sun. I looked down, painfully aware of the gap between us. When I looked up, the driver was gone.

Sometimes I'd wondered what would happen if the rich girl climbed from her car to speak to me instead of sticking her head out of the window, then retreating into the safety of her AC. Now she was beside me and I could feel her waiting for me to speak.

Chapter 6

'I didn't think cars like this could break down.'

I looked at the car, trying to see it through the hawker's eyes. It is shiny and big and black, almost monstrous when compared with some of the things on the road.

'I suppose there's a first time for everything.'

The sack balanced on his head dripped water down his face. I followed a droplet as it slid down his temple. It was held up by an anomalous spot before rolling under his chin and disappearing into his shirt.

'How was school?'

'Eh?'

'How was school?'

'It was fine. How was hawking today?'

'Fine.'

The next silence seemed less awkward.

'How old are you?'

'Seventeen,' I said.

'I guessed so.'

'How?'

'I don't know. You just look like a seventeen-year-old.'

'How old are you?'

'Eighteen.'

'I guessed so too.'

He smiled and his white teeth suddenly contrasted with his skin.

'Do you enjoy hawking?'

He made a 'Mm' sound.

'Have you been hawking for long?'

He nodded but said nothing.

'How did you become a hawker?'

He opened his mouth then he shut it.

'You don't have to say if you don't want to.'

'No it's not that. I . . .'

His words trailed off. Maybe this was not going to work. Hassan could not have gone far. If I called him, he would be back in five minutes. One last try then I was leaving.

'We can sit on the car and talk.'

'What about this?' He pointed at the bag of ice cream propped against his thigh.

I hoisted it up. It was heavier and colder than I expected but I continued. 'This can come with us.'

I set it on the bonnet, which had cooled, and climbed on in what I hoped was a delicate but unconsciously seductive manner. I waited to see if he would follow. Finally he said, 'If a customer drives by I'll have to go.'

'OK,' I said, leaning backwards on to the windscreen. 'So back to how you became a hawker.'

✳ ✳ ✳

Intermittently he would jump down to chase after a car, re-turning with a fraction of what I had in my wallet. He spoke pidgin to some of his customers but the English he used with me was confident and without traces of the grammar you expect from drivers, hawkers, etcetera. His manners too were those of a host. He offered me an ice cream and when I tried to pay, he waved my money away. I was even glad he had been reluctant to speak to me at first. It was the natural reaction to someone he had only known for two and a half weeks.

'Where was I,' he said for what seemed like the fiftieth time that afternoon.

'You were just going to tell me about your aunty.'

'Yes. Aunty Precious. She is my— I think your driver is back.'

Behind Hassan trailed a man in oil-stained overalls.

'Aunty, this is the mechanic.'

'Good afternoon.'

We slid off the car front to let him look inside. Leaning in, he shook his head and made a clicking sound.

'What's the matter?'

'The carburettor.'

I played along.

'Can you fix it?'

'I will try my best. It might take me some time.'

For ten minutes, I watched the quack bang a spanner in the hood of my car. Finally he slammed the bonnet shut and said,

'Test it.'

As expected, the car hummed beautifully.

'How much?'

'Fifteen hundred.'

We both knew that there was nothing wrong with my jeep. Yet arguing over money with this ragged man would not look good. I brought out my wallet and counted out the sum.

As Hassan started the car I remembered something.

'What's your name?'

After he told me, I waited for him to ask for mine. When he didn't, I wound up my window and nodded to Hassan. It probably wouldn't have been worth it. After all he is a hawker.

'What's yours?'

I slid the window down again.

'Abikẹ. Abikẹ Johnson.'

The first proper sentence I say to her and the only thing I could think of was 'I didn't think cars like this could break down.'

She was taller than I'd expected. In the back seat she looked small and young; I would have placed her age at no more than fifteen. Outside, she stood without awkwardness and the small breasts under her shirt were carried with ease.

That first time I saw her, she had been a vision after the sweat and grime of the road. The more she stopped and rolled down her window, the more unsure I became of her looks. As I studied her now I was almost certain she was not pretty. Still there was a quality to her face, an edge that would make her stand out in a line of much better-looking girls.

* * *

'How was hawking today?'

'How old are you?'

'Do you enjoy hawking?'

I wondered what she saw when she looked at me: a boy in cracked shoes, an ice-cream seller, a strange creature to be prodded with her questions.

'Have you been hawking for long?'

'How did you become a hawker?'

Her insistence was beginning to grate.

'You don't have to say if you don't want to.'

It would be better for both of us if I found an excuse to leave. I reached for my sack but her fingers were there before mine. Brushing my hand away she picked it up, placed it on the hood and climbed on. Until this moment, she had been a lonely girl in a large car. If I thought it odd that she only bought ice cream from me, though up to six of us might flock to her window, I didn't let it bother me. If I thought she smiled too much when we spoke and looked in my eyes too little, I put it down to shyness. As I watched her climb on to the car it struck me. All this time she had been flirting. Despite my shabby clothes and sweaty body, for some reason this increasingly attractive girl was flirting with me!

'If a customer drives by, I'll have to go,' I said in a feeble attempt to regain control.

'OK. So, back to how you became a hawker.'

At this point I should have said, No, tell me a bit about yourself, but I was flattered. For the next hour, when I wasn't selling ice cream, I spoke about myself.

'I've been hawking for about two years now.'
'That means you were sixteen when you started.'
'Yes. I started really late. Most of the guys had been hawking for years by the time I joined.'
'What were you doing before?'
'Other things.'
A battered Peugeot pulled up beside us. 'Bros, are you a big man or a hawker?'
'Wetin you want?'
'Abeg give me one ice cream.'
'Hundred naira.'
'Give me for eighty.'
'Hundred last price.'
Before we could exchange, traffic moved.
'Excuse me.'
I jumped down with my sack.

When I came back, she was leaning against the windscreen, her legs stretching the length of the bonnet, her feet dangling over its edges.
'Sorry about that. Where were we?'
'We were talking about what you did before hawking.'
I placed the sack between us and returned to my former position.
'Before I started hawking I thought it was a simple thing.

You find some sweets, find a road and start selling.'

'What else is there?'

'A lot. You need to consider the type of traffic on the road, the type of cars, the kind of people—'

'Ssss!'

A woman in a red Toyota was beckoning.

'Excuse me.'

When I returned, the leg closest to me had slid up, making a triangle of her calf, her thigh and the shiny black metal of the hood.

'Sorry about that.'

'It's OK.'

'Would you like an ice cream?'

She nodded and brought out her wallet.

'Don't worry.'

The one I chose for her was from the bottom. Just holding the wrapper numbed my fingers. For myself, I chose a runny ice cream at the top: an acquired taste.

'So was hawking difficult when you first started?'

'Very, very difficult.'

'How come?'

'It was different from anything I'd done before.'

Biting into the plastic, I squeezed the bottom and spurted cold, sweet, milk on to my tongue. Beside me, she nibbled a small opening in the corner and squeezed a few drops into her mouth.

'I wasn't used to shouting Buy This and Buy That in the middle of a road. You should have seen what I was like a few years ago. If you'd known me, you wouldn't have thought I'd be able to do this job.'

'I wonder what you were like.'

A little girl in the backseat of a Benz caught my eye.

'I'm really sorry. Excuse me.'

It went on like this for the whole hour. A snippet of conversation about myself, a customer calling, my running and returning breathless, another snippet, a customer, running, breathless, until the driver came back and she left and the only things I knew about her were her name, her age and her laugh. Her tongue snakes out, her head rolls back, her mouth is sliced to reveal small, immaculate teeth. Surprisingly, the sound released is mellow.

Chapter 7

I didn't become a hawker straight away. Six months after my father died, we moved to Mile 12 and Uncle Kayode, one of his friends, found me a place at a local school. He could not afford my private school fees nor could he find me a job if I had no SSCE results. The place at the government school was a compromise. 'Manage it for two years,' he said. 'After you graduate, we'll see what we can do.'

It was an all-boys school, old, prestigious, some famous Nigerians had been there in its glory days. During assembly I could not take my eyes off the crumbling buildings. In my first lesson, I used my lap for a desk and spent the whole hour straining to hear the teacher. Her voice was too quiet for the one hundred and twenty of us stuffed into that room.

I lasted three months. By that time, I was beginning to see that the largesse of my father's friends would run out. It was one of my classmates that steered me to my current profession. He was bragging of a friend who made 'good money' from selling sweets on the road. He clammed up once I tried to find out more.

None of my classmates liked me. I was curt, I sneered at their grammar, I faked an American twang, anything to show I was different. At break time, instead of joining their football matches, I would wander to the edge of the playing fields and remember my old school where only twenty of us sat in a class with unbroken tables and chairs.

I blamed my father bitterly on those afternoons. He was too weak to tell his glamorous wife that he could not afford the gold she was so fond of and the annual trips abroad. I imagined him borrowing to feed her cravings for luxury, our cravings for luxury. There was a time Jọkẹ and I would only eat restaurant food. And then there were his relatives who were always at our house asking for money. Sometimes the same man would come three times in a week and each time he would leave with a brown envelope.

'He's my cousin,' I heard him say to my mother once.

'Is that why you had to give him all the money in the house?'

'He needed it for his school fees.'

'He's been in that university for eight years now. What kind of degree is that?'

'Darling, I've told you before. In my whole family, I am the most successful so I must give back the most.'

He must have been heavily in debt when he died. This was why it all fell apart so easily.

Since my classmate wouldn't tell me how to become a hawker, I decided to find out for myself. Every morning I would drop Jọkẹ at school, pick a road at random and start a conversation with a hawker to find out where he got the goods. At first they mistrusted me. My pidgin was faltering; I spoke too loudly, enunciated too slowly. Some said I should go to the expensive Stop and Buy. 'Everything we get,' one said, 'they also get am for there.' I smiled at that. Even I was not so naive.

Eventually Wednesday, a Mile 12 hawker, told me the truth. They got the sweets from large wholesalers and took home only fifteen per cent of what they sold. When I first heard how paltry the commission was, I laughed and offended him. Surely, he had to be a little mad to work ten hours a day, seven days a week for a sum my mother used to spend on a packet of Kellogg's Cornflakes.

I chose my road carefully. It wasn't too small, it wasn't too dirty, it had an adequate amount of traffic. What I failed to note was the type of traffic my seemingly perfect location had. It was a *danfo* route and not many people who had spare cash to buy sweets entered these cramped yellow and black buses.

My first mistake was forgivable. I was new to the job. I could change location. My second was more serious. I wouldn't hawk. I could not overcome the indignity of shouting 'Buy Mentos!' to a road full of people. On the rare occasion someone beckoned, I would saunter over with a slight irritation in my face and I never, ever, ran. I would rather lose a customer than chase after him.

It was a woman in one of these *danfos* who pointed me in the right direction. She was sitting at the window seat with her head drooping out. When she saw me looking she smiled. Usually, when people wanted my attention they hissed. I shambled to her side.

'Which sweet do you want?'

'You should try. When I see you frowning under this sun I feel sorry for you.'

'Pardon?'

'Hawking like this won't help you. Smile sometimes, come and stand on the road more often and try.'

She smiled again, this time a smaller, more natural smile, then traffic relented and her head was gone.

Later that day a man crooked his finger at me. Before I could reach him, the bus started moving. I turned to walk back to my place on the side of the road. I had tried. Then I turned back. The *danfo* was fifty metres ahead of me and it was gathering speed.

I ran.

Hurtling on to the highway with a clear stretch ahead of it, no traffic to slow it down, moving ten metres to my one step. I ran. Futile, pointless, impossible, you didn't have to tell me any of this; the fact I could just see the number plate was enough. And then I ran some more. I ran after that bus like someone inside was going to buy my entire rack. I ran after the bus until I couldn't see it any more.

I took home seventy-five naira that day. After chasing ten cars and selling five hundred naira's worth of sweets, I could not even buy a loaf of bread. That night I worked out that I had to sell two thousand naira's worth of product everyday to make hawking worth my while. I changed to a road with traffic lights to get a wider variety of customers. I added ten naira to the price if the customer was in a new Toyota; twenty if they were in a Mercedes. Still, even with sales more than trebled, I never took home more than four hundred naira.

I was about to tell Abikẹ about Aunty Precious and how she helped me when the driver returned with a mechanic. This mechanic charged her 1500 naira for a spanner twist and a few drops of engine oil. She didn't bother to haggle though it was clear he was asking for at least triple the normal price. Is she really so naïve or was she just trying to impress me? I don't like either answer.

Chapter 8

Three weeks ago, I wouldn't have believed I'd soon be sitting on a roadside talking to a hawker like an old friend. Yet here I was returning home after spending an hour with this boy, wishing my driver had stayed away longer. As we drove up to the entrance, Hassan became nervous. He is afraid of the two armed guards that stand in front of my gate, which is impenetrable to certain types of missile.

'Please no let them point their gun at me.'

'They wouldn't dare with me here.'

The first guard swaggered to the car and flashed his torch at my driver's face. Hassan shrank under the glare, his head almost touching the steering wheel.

'Good evening, sah.'

How dare they bully my driver when they knew I was in the car? My window slid down.

'Turn off that torch. What do you want?'

'Why are you just coming back from school?'

'Open the gate.'

His partner called from where he was standing. 'You no go

give us answer?'

'*Open this gate now.*'

'*Your father said we should ask why you come late.*'

'*You have asked me.*'

The guard by my car spoke into his walkie-talkie and the gate rolled open.

He was asking about me because it was Wednesday. Wednesday is the only day my father will see petitioners. It is also by silent agreement the day we meet for sparring. It was clumsy of me to forget. I should have planned the breakdown for tomorrow.

'Hassan, drop me in his study.'

Standing two storeys high, with a rooftop swimming pool, my father's 'study' is not the expected room filled with books. He comes here to meet guests secretly. I am the only one of his children allowed inside. When I came to his actual study, Mr Dosunmu was standing outside the door.

'Good evening, Abikẹ.'

I cannot pinpoint what Mr Dosunmu is to my father. Right-hand man would suggest dependence. Maybe stooge. He looks like a stooge. Short and pot-bellied with a silent manner that makes him seem smaller.

'He is in a meeting.'

Without knocking, I pushed the door open. My father bared his teeth when he saw me, the birthmark on his temple stretching with his lips.

'This is my daughter Abikẹ.'

The man opposite him turned. When he nodded at me, I

nodded back, holding his gaze. I have no respect for people who choose to play games with my father.

'So we have finished our discussion for the day?'

'But, Mr Johnson, what about—'

'We have finished our discussion for the day. Leave anything extra with Dosunmu.'

My father stood and extended his hand.

'I must say that—'

'This has been a most pleasant meeting,' my father completed. 'You need say no more. Really.'

The man jerked upright. There was something in the 'really' that forbade discussion. They shook hands, my father's hand doing all the gripping, the other hand barely participating. When he dragged his feet out, my father and I were left alone. I remained standing.

'So, Abike, where have you been?'

He knew.

'That's all you know about her? After an hour?'

'Mr T, it might seem small to you but it's quite important. She has a nice laugh so she must be a happy person and she's seventeen so . . .' I trailed off. 'What kind of guy talks about himself for an hour? I wonder what she thinks of me. Next time—'

'*If* there is a next time. She might be tired of you.' He sounded almost annoyed.

'Don't worry. There will be a next time. How can she resist all my second-hand glory?'

'Boy, you buy your clothes from Yaba. Third-hand is

closer to the truth.'

'I have to go. Aunty Precious will be waiting.'

I patted the cardboard by his hand and walked to the road that led to *Aunty Precious* BLESSED FOOD STORES.

I entered the shop just under a year ago looking for a better deal. At first I tried to buy from my wholesaler to sell on at a profit but I was told my quantities were too small. So with ten months of savings, I left the warehouse and started my search for a shop owner who would split fifty per cent of their cost price and give me sixty per cent of the profit. After all, I would be the one running in the sun.

No one was interested. You had to be desperate to even consider such terms. For three weeks, I tramped through the streets of Lagos, starting with the largest retailers – where I was not even allowed to see the manager – and working my way down to the smallest shops that were little more than kiosks. None were desperate enough.

I wandered into *Aunty Precious* BLESSED FOOD STORES by chance. It was a wonder I even noticed the squat building that had faded into the colour of the dust strip that encircled it. It had two storeys and, as was often the case, only the ground floor was a shop. Above, tenants aired themselves and their faded clothing on their balconies.

'Hello?'

I stood at the doorway, blocking the sunlight and peering into the dim room. There was nobody at the till. I glanced at the four aisles of goods and the small freezer humming in the background. The place wasn't dusty, or dirty or untidy.

In fact, everything was neatly arranged, the products lined up in barrack-straight rows. Still you could tell business was slow.

'Hello?' I said again, walking to the end of the shop. The shelves were stocked with tinned food, detergent, tooth-paste, bread, cereal and, against the wall, a freezer crammed with ice cream. In the last aisle, I saw a woman sound asleep on a stool. Her body sagged round the stool seat, allowing her to balance without leaning on anything. The hem of her starched *boubou* swept the floor, the skin of her round face relaxed around her jaws. On the white scarf wrapped around her head were the words 'women's prayer conference 2006' printed in bold. I cleared my throat loudly and she opened eyes that were large with sleep.

'You must be Aunty Precious.'

'Yes. And who are you?'

'I'm a hawker,' I said, reducing my volume to match hers.

'You don't look like one.'

'Yes and this is because, today, I come as something more than a hawker. I come as—'

'If you're here to sell me something let me remind you that you are in a shop.'

'I know. And this is why I'm here because—'

'And if you've come to buy anything from me, I'll give you some advice. It's cheaper at a wholesaler's. Wait, I'll write an address for you.'

When she stood, I saw she would have been petite if not for

the weight that gathered round her hips. She walked to the front desk and wrote on a piece of paper.

'Thank you very much. This is not what I came for,' I said, tucking the slip into my pocket.

'Then why are you here?'

'I have a business proposal.'

'Why didn't you say so?'

I was well rehearsed by now. I had made my proposal almost ten times that day and each time it sounded more natural. I delivered my pitch with my hands behind my back, making eye contact half of the time.

'And so,' I said, rounding up, 'this is why I know it would be in your best interest to become my partner.'

'Why do I need you? How do you know I'm not happy with my profit?'

'You might be happy but you'd be happier if you made more. Also, your business needs to be taken to the next level.'

'Why do I need to be taken to the next level?'

'Because you are not – are not maximising your potential.'

'And how do you know this?'

'Because:

'There are few gaps on the shelves.

'The products are too neatly arranged for people to have shopped here recently.

'The floor is clean. Customers would have brought dirt in.'

She laughed, a low, throaty laugh that bore no relation to her appearance. 'I'm impressed. I'd be even more impressed if there wasn't a flyer in the window announcing the store is closing in two months.'

I walked outside the store and looked at the window. There it was. A large red poster saying in black block letters: CLOSING IN TWO MONTHS.

'You're a good boy,' she said when I came back in. 'As you *now* know, my shop is closing down. Neither of us can stop that from happening but I will hire you for the eight weeks I have left.'

'Thank you. You won't regret this.'

'Eight weeks only. Is there anything you want to ask?'

'Since the shop is well-stocked, why don't I start hawking some of the things you have now? We can split the profits sixty–forty. Of course you would be taking the sixty per cent.'

If she didn't agree, it would be the end. No one was going to consider my offer. I knew that now. The wholesalers wouldn't take me back. I would go home and spend my savings on Dettol, soap, cereal and bread. In fact I didn't have to go home. I could spend them here.

'How about you take fifty per cent since you're the one running on the road.'

✴ ✴ ✴

I was thinking about this first meeting when I arrived at the store today. Eleven months later it's still open. For this I must take some credit, though the office that opened down the road also has something to do with its solvency. I read the sign outside and as usual, it made me smile. On one side was written in pink, italic letters: *Aunty Precious* and on the other side in cramped block letters: BLESSED FOOD STORES. Coming from one direction, you could be walking past a beauty salon or, when it was night and the script blazed into the dark neighbourhood, a brothel. Coming the other way, it was a shop that sold olive oil and locust paste.

When I walked in, Aunty Precious was sobbing at the till and a strange ox of a man was on his knees. They both looked at me. Her face was tear-streaked, her eyes swollen into two red moons. The strange man looked like he was about to cry.

'Emeka, you have to leave,' Aunty Precious said to him.

'But—'

'Please leave me.'

'Pre—'

'I'm sorry, sir, but madam said you have to go.'

He looked at Aunty Precious. She turned her face. When he walked out with his eyes fixed to the floor, she put her head down on the till and continued sobbing.

'Aunty Precious, what's wrong?'

Chapter 9

'So, Abikẹ, where have you been?'

My father rarely asks such a direct question without knowing the answer.

'The car had a fault so Hassan went to fetch a mechanic.'

He was standing but the distance between us made it seem like we were level. Tall, without being thickset; handsome without effeminacy: physically, most would say he is perfect. I have always thought there is a worrying sharpness about him.

'What about this friend of yours?' I had seen the IG many times in this study. Perhaps my father was now using his network.

'Oh, the hawker? He's just someone I buy stuff from. He's very handsome though.'

I knew the last part would annoy him. He is like a normal father in some respects.

'I'm not sure this is the kind of person you should be spending time with.'

He had stopped asking questions.

'What do you mean?' I asked, picking up a leather-bound book that was lying on the cabinet. Crime and Punishment, I *read off the spine.*

'Abikẹ, you know perfectly well what I mean.'

I put the tome down, smiling at the fingerprints I'd left on its dusty surface.

'Well, usually I would agree but there's something special about this hawker.'

I turned my back to him, facing the trophy cabinet where he kept his accolades, the yellow lighting caressing the oiled metals. *Best Student: King's College, 1974,* I read off a recent addition.

'You mean he's handsome.'

My eyes darted to the image of him reflected in the cabinet glass. He was standing under a painting of himself and both pairs of eyes were looking into my back.

'Yes,' I replied, waiting for the reflection's mouth to open before adding, 'Also because there's something odd about him. He doesn't look like he belongs to "our kind" yet he acts like it.'

'Don't be naive. Anyone can pick up posh manners.'

'Like you, Daddy?' I asked, turning to stare directly into his face.

He is very proud of the fact that no classmate of his has ever recognised him. The Olu Johnson we know and love has come a long way from Olumide Jolomijo of fifty years ago.

'Yes, like me, Abikẹ.'

'Well, Daddy, don't you think that someone smart enough to reinvent themselves deserves some curiosity? Like you.'

He smiled as we sat.

Mr Johnson: 1

Abikẹ: 1

'So who was that?'

'A Lagosian Senator.'

'Why did he come?'

'He is looking for a rather large amount of money to rig the next election.'

'What did you tell him?'

'Yes.'

'And if he doesn't win?'

'I'm sponsoring his rival.'

In the stories he selects for me, he is always the wily fox; rarely brutal or cruel. It shows he values my opinion. He of all people should know better.

'So, Abikẹ, why are the windows of my newest jeep still not tinted?'

Because how will my hawker see me when I drive past?

'Because only government officials are allowed tinted windows in Lagos. Besides, it saves money.'

'My money.'

'Not forever.'

'I do have other children.'

'But you want Johnson Corporations to succeed when you're dead.'

Abikẹ: 2

Mr Johnson: 1

We continued like this but the score remained the same. By the end of the evening, I had won. As usual, we went through the

Wednesday ritual of a robust hug. I often tell myself, while he crushes me, that Frustration is his way of preparing me for the world. Playing becomes easier if I believe the game doesn't stem from perverseness.

'Abikẹ, I'd like to meet this hawker of yours.'

I hugged him back, my arms unable to exert a pressure his thick hide would feel.

'Why not? I'll invite him over sometime. Maybe one of these days you'll run into each other.'

As usual, it ended in a draw.

I looked at Aunty Precious's heaving shoulders. She had not answered me.

'Aunty Precious, what's wrong?'

'Nothing,' she mumbled, her head still buried in the crook of her arm.

'Who was that?'

'Nobody.'

'What's wrong?'

'Nothing. I'm fine. Just go.'

'I don't want to leave you alone.'

'Go. Your mother and sister will be worried.'

She was leaning stiffly against the wall when I left, eyes closed, like a person who had fainted in a sitting position. It was a relief to step into the evening breeze. My mood soon sank when I remembered where I was going. Even the garbage wants to escape from my neighbourhood. At the end of each day, people pile their rubbish on to the side of the road and the next morning, you see the sweet wrappers and banana skins a few metres from where you left them, slowly being carried to their freedom by people's unsuspecting feet. Oh, to be trash.

As I turned into my street, I was disgusted by the ugliness that even moonlight could not soften. The rubbish heaps that looked like burial mounds; the candlelit house fronts that shed light on scenes made uglier by the flickering jaundiced glow cast on them: melon-bellied children chasing a lame dog with sticks, a man squatting in the shadows, showing solidarity by shitting pellets into his neighbour's compound.

I don't know why people in my area get robbed. All our valuables put together and trebled would still be a fraction of what thieves could get from some of the houses I can think of. Whatever their logic, the armed robbers pay us a visit twice a month. We hear the gunshots, we cower and the next day we thank God it wasn't us. There's no talk of calling the police. We're not their type.

We are luckier than most to have a two-bedroom flat all to ourselves. My father's leftover money combined with the sporadic generosity of his old colleagues and friends was enough to pay rent for five years. The lease contract is in a drawer in my mother's room. Sometimes I wonder what will happen when it runs out. I have some money saved, but it is for the shop I want to start.

As usual, when I got home, there were boys smoking on the bench by the stairwell, the tips of their sticks glowing red in the dark.

'Boyo, how far?' my neighbour's fifteen-year-old son said, in a fake gruff voice.

'Good evening, Ayo.'

'I don tell you. My name be Rambo. You wan smoke?' he said, offering me something that was too fat to be a cigarette.

'No, thank you.'

When we first moved in, Ayo was the only boy in our block I approved of Jọkẹ speaking to. He went to school every day, he combed his hair every morning and he knew what he wanted to study in university.

'If you no want smoke gerrout from here.'

A year ago I would have told Ayo to show some more respect. Ever since I saw him smash a bottle over a boy's head in a fight, I have grown wary of him.

When I walked into our flat, my mother was sitting in the living room where I had left her. At least she wasn't in her nightie.

'Mummy, good evening.'

'Welcome.'

'How was your day?'

She looked at the table as if bewildered to find herself still sitting there. 'It was good, I think.'

I walked into the room I shared with Jọkẹ.

'Jọkẹ, I'm back.'

'OK.'

There was a candle next to the bed and she was doing her homework on her lap.

'Has Mummy eaten?'

'I don't know.'

This is how she is at home: curt, monosyllabic.

'Have you eaten?'

'I made noodles.'

'Why didn't you make for Mummy?'

'I cooked them for her once and she said they looked like worms.'

I went out again.

'Mummy, what do you want to eat?'

She stood and began to walk towards the kitchen. 'That is what I should be asking you. Do you want yam pottage?'

The last time she tried to cook supper, Jọkẹ and I were out. When we came back, there was smoke in the apartment and a pot on the stove, burnt to black uselessness.

I led her back to the chair. 'No, thank you. I've already eaten. What about you?'

'Maybe a little bread.'

I spread margarine over a slice and waited until she had swallowed her first bite before returning to the room.

'Jọkẹ, next time make sure she starts eating before you leave.'

'OK.'

'Or if it's not too much to ask, you can sit with her while she eats.'

'OK.'

'And you can say something other than OK.'

'OK.'

When I went outside, my mother was still nibbling on the

white part, her teeth sinking into the bread a millimetre at a time.

Three months after he died, while we still had one car left and my mother was alert enough to drive it, she took me to the accident site and pointed at the blackened chassis of what had been my father's car. Already the grass was beginning to reclaim it, growing round its geometric shape. We parked and walked down the slope.

'It is empty,' my mother said as I stuck my hand through a gaping window, clenching and unclenching my fist. My father was the only padding that had stood between life and a blackened skeleton, between before and after.

Sometimes, I search my memories for a clip of before and play it to myself. A favourite is the first time I saw snow. I was in New York and it was not snow like you saw in the movies. It was brown and gritty like sand.

'What is it?' I asked my father.

'Snow.'

'No,' Jọkẹ said. 'Snow is white.'

'It stings,' said my mother, 'cover your eyes.'

Now it seems a lie that, once upon a time, my father's bank account was full enough for the American embassy to grant us visas. But it is true. I have been to America. There are stamps in my expired passport to prove it. I have seen snow. For this there is no proof except the memories in my head. They are enough to remind me that once I knew more than Mile 12 and hawking and fetching water on Friday evenings.

It was before Abikẹ wanted to know about when she was asking all those questions.

I don't share.

Chapter 10

'Do you want to come to my house this weekend?'

'Pardon?'

'Would you like to come to my house on Saturday?'

'Well, I—'

'Some friends are coming over and I thought you might like to come.'

I worried about inviting him. The papers are always full of armed robbers who are hawkers in the daytime.

'Yeah, sure. What's your address?'

Even if he is a thief, it is unlikely that he and his gang will get past my gate.

'It's fine. We'll pick you up at one o'clock?'

'That's really nice, Abiké. I'll be here.'

It's possible my father is right. The speech and manners may be newly acquired. Or worse, the road may make him seem more polished than he is. If he doesn't come to my house, I'll never know if he can fit into my life.

'Don't be late.'
'Same to you.'

'The prophet said I would know.'

'Know what?'

'I will just know.'

More and more this prophet kept appearing in our conversations, his robes brushing our faces, his sandalled feet treading on our toes.

'Tell me about the prophet.'

I shouldn't have encouraged him. Once you go back further than two years with Mr T, he loses his lucidity, perhaps even a portion of his sanity. But I wanted to know what was hidden behind this character that he could not stop mentioning.

'The prophet was a man that helped me through a bad time. Though not for free.' He chuckled. 'Nothing is free in Lagos.'

'Surely a good prophet would not collect money for his prophecies.'

'Shut up!' he shouted, striking the cardboard we were sitting on. 'You don't know what you are speaking of. Besides, I didn't need what I gave him.'

'What did you give him?'

'My hand.'

'Your what?'

Suddenly I did not want to know the rest of this story, did not even want to know if it were true. He mistook my silence for interest.

'I was wandering through the bush one day and I came upon him. He was standing absolutely still with his hands raised to the sky like this.'

He raised his good arm to the bridge, his gaunt fingers brushing the air.

'I was in the bush because that's where I buried my daughter. I carried her body four thousand steps outside Lagos. She was beginning to smell or I would have gone the full six thousand: a – a thousand for every year.'

There were many questions that could kick holes in this new fabrication of his: how did you keep your hand fresh but not your daughter? Why did you carry your fresh hand to your daughter's funeral?

'In the end I couldn't even bury her. Try using one hand to dig a hole.'

I laughed, a short bark of a thing that left me feeling ashamed. This story could have been ripped from a home video: horror that melted into tragedy that swung into farce with the delivery of a line. Still, imagined or not, it was real to him, more real than the bridge he lived under.

'I'm sorry.'

'Don't be. I should be laughed at. Mr T the hero, marching off with my daughter slung over my shoulder. I should just have placed her in the ocean. It would have been better than the hole I couldn't even cover properly.'

He was mumbling now, speaking to himself.

'If I had put her in the ocean I would never have met the prophet and the prophet would never have given me the prophecy and I wouldn't be alive now, because the only thing keeping me alive—'

'So what was the prophet's name?'

'The man who cut it off told me to keep it and sell it. But the prophet's prophecy was more valuable than mere naira.'

'What did he say?'

'He said I would know when she came.'

'Who?'

'An exchange.'

'What?'

He hissed. 'You should not ask what you do not want to know.'

He was right.

'I'm going to buy some *chin-chin*. Do you want?'

'No thank you.'

I walked to one of the women who made it their business to provide finger food to the scum of Lagos. They sold under the lurid film posters that were plastered all over Abẹ Bridge. Why did they choose here, when their wooden tables could barely fit into the small space for pedestrians, when local street children buzzed around, looking for an opportunity to snatch and run, when most of their customers were men like me and Mr T?

'Thank you, Aunty,' I said, when she poured an extra cup of *chin-chin* into my bag.

'No problem, my son.'

She was fat, like most of the women traders, their rolling flesh the best advert for their goods.

'Buy biscuit!' a particularly large one called out and before you knew it a round of Buy cake! and Buy buns! was heard under the bridge.

'So how are things with your friend? Abikẹ something,'
 'Johnson,' I said, pouring some *chin-chin* into Mr T's lap. 'She asked me to come to her house this Saturday.'
 'Finally, a breakthrough.'
 It was a strange choice of words. One I would have commented on if I hadn't caught sight of my cracked shoes.
 'I don't have anything to wear.'
 'What's wrong with what you're wearing now? It's better than what I have on.'
 'I can't wear this. Imagine me in her house wearing this.'
 'I think you look fine.'

When I got home I searched my cupboards for something presentable. Everything was too small.
 'Jọkẹ, what do you think?'
 She shook her head.
 'Mummy, what do you think?'
 'You know everything looks good on you.'

Aunty Precious proved more helpful. When I told her about Saturday, she offered to help me choose an outfit. At first I was uncomfortable. The only woman I'd ever been shopping with was my mother. I soon settled into the routine of sifting through the mounds of clothing and occasionally asking her opinion.

We had come to Yaba market, the home of cheap wooden stalls bowed under the weight of the average Nigerian's need to look Western for as Eastern a price as possible. The stalls were jammed together, clothes flung together, people squashed together, sifting, lifting, arranging without thought to compatibility. If only I had grown up not knowing better then I wouldn't feel degraded coming here.

'So, who is this girl?'

'Pardon?'

'I said who is this girl that is worth all this trouble?'

'How do you know it's a girl?'

'How about this?'

I looked at the green shirt with POLO RALPH LOREN stencilled across the front. Maybe Aunty Precious hadn't noticed but Abikẹ certainly would.

'Too bright.'

'What's her name?'

'Abikẹ.'

'Abikẹ who?'

'Johnson.'

'What did you say her father's name was?'

'I don't know, Mr Johnson I guess? Are you all right?' She was clutching the shirt to her chest and breathing heavily.

'Aunty Precious—'

Before I could ask who she thought Abikẹ's father was, the stall owner interrupted.

'Madam, no rumple my cloth.'

'Sorry, don't mind me. See I don fold am for you.'

She folded the shirt and then others that people had

placed carelessly.

'Stop looking so concerned. I'm OK. You can't know this girl very well if you don't even know her father's name. Where are you going?'

'Her house.'

'She must be bold to ask you out.'

'I don't think it's a date.'

'Of course it's a date. You have to match her boldness.'

She held a shirt against me. There was a small tremor in her hand but it was not marked enough for me to comment.

'It's pink,' I said, looking at the shirt for the first time.

'She'll love it.'

Chapter 11

I nearly drove past him. I've only ever seen him in greys and once whites. It didn't occur to me that the boy in the hot pink shirt could be my hawker until he waved. I would have laughed at anyone else but the shirt looked new or at least seldom worn.

'Hi,' he said, when he climbed into the car and he didn't say much until we reached the gates. There, the guards tried to embarrass me. Despite the bright sunshine, they flashed their torches into my driver's face. Then the beam was directed at us.

'Who is there?'

The buffoon. Couldn't he see me in the back of the car? Wasn't that enough to guarantee anyone else?

'Please open these gates. I don't have time for this.'

'We need to know every person that enters this house.'

'Whose house is it?' That silenced him. 'Put Abikẹ and friend on your list. Open these gates.'

'Your daddy said—'

'Now, please.'

* * *

How dare they speak me like that in front of a guest? I turned to see my guest frowning.

'Those gatemen.' I said.

'They were just doing their jobs.'

Clearly, he thought I was the employer's daughter abusing my position.

'You know, you may be right.'

There were some things I could not expect him to sympathise with.

'Hmm,' he said, but the look was gone.

I showed him parts of the house and, to his credit, he appeared only mildly impressed. The gym, the tennis courts, even the indoor swimming pool, none could get a reaction more overstated than 'You have a really nice house, Abikẹ.' We ended up alone in my living room. As the minutes passed and he didn't speak, I grew uncomfortable. Was he bored? Should I switch on the TV or chat? What would we talk about? How does a hawker speak so well? Too direct. Are you enjoying yourself? Too patronising.

'So who else is coming, Abikẹ?'

'Are you afraid it's just going to be the two of us?'

He didn't respond.

'Don't worry, there are other people coming.'

'That's cool.'

Why was it cool?

'Not that I would mind if it were just the two of us.'

'Well, it's not.'

I hadn't meant to snap. 'Their names are Cynthia and

Oritṣe,' I said in a more even tone. 'They're old friends.'

'Do they know I'm a hawker?'

They might not act naturally if they knew.

'Does it matter?'

'Do you think it matters, Abikẹ?'

Before I could answer they arrived and the moment was lost. Or paused.

'Cynthia. Oritṣe. You guys are late. This is my friend—'

He stood and introduced himself. When he shook Cynthia's hand, she held on for longer than was necessary. Oritṣe on the other hand tried to out-shake him and withdrew flexing his fingers. With his crisp shirt and starched trousers, Oritṣe looked silly when put beside my hawker. Having only been invited to my house, there was no need for the designer sunglasses balanced on his head. And of course he kept looking for my approval. To everything he said would be added the question: 'Abikẹ, what do you think?' or 'Don't you agree?' Abikẹ, Abikẹ, Abikẹ after every single sentence.

My hawker didn't need validation.

'No, Abikẹ. How can you say that Tobe's second album was better than his first? Don't you remember "Nasco Love"?'

'That song about cornflakes was so stupid. There's no one good in Nigerian music at the moment. Don't you agree, Abikẹ?'

'Nasco cornflakes love,' my hawker sang completely out of tune.

'Just add milk and sugar and we're ready to go,' I sang back. 'Nasco cornflakes love.'

'She doesn't stress me. She's no aristo.'
We laughed, just the two of us.
'So you agree the first album was better.'
'Maybe.'
'But, Abikẹ, don't you think—'

Oritse and I, well from my point of view there was never an Oritse and I. I keep him around because his voice is special. Cynthia has been a member of my set for the longest, I think. She has no real gifts but she is very beautiful in that plump way. More importantly, she is obedient.

After the meal had been cleared away and Oritse had sung, my hawker was the first to say he had to leave. The other two remained sprawled on my sofa, refusing to take his lead.

'Cynthia, Oritse, are you coming?'

Their drivers were waiting outside but there was no driver for my hawker.

'Thanks, Abikẹ. We'll see later,' was all he said by way of goodbye. I watched him walk down the drive. Even with his long strides, it would take him at least ten minutes to reach the gates. I watched until all I could see was a pink blob. When I turned to go inside, I realised the colour had grown on me.

I'm not sure what I thought of the day.

At first it was as awkward as I'd expected. Once I stepped into the jeep I began to feel uncomfortable. Her strong perfume filled the air and her legs strayed over the divider whenever the car went over a bump. When I placed my hand on the slippery leather seat to relax myself, my fingers crushed the yellow cotton of her dress. I felt her staring at my tough, chipped nails.

'How was school yesterday?'

'It was fine. How was work?'

'It was fine.'

The hum of the air conditioning filled the silence until we reached the gates of her house. There, my discomfort intensified. Many houses have gates in Lagos but even the highest gates I've seen look like entrances. They have knockers, they have slits for gatemen to peer through and ask, 'Who is that?' This gate was a slab of metal, without contours, or knobs or anything you could hold on to. It looked like a dead end; a sign that whoever was in the car should turn back. There was barbed wire everywhere, jagged protrusions that would slice the skin of any man who tried to scale the Johnson entrance. And if, somehow, your thickness still stopped you from understanding you were not wanted, there were two armed guards to drive home the point.

One of the guards approached. He was an oldish man who held his gun uncomfortably, almost timidly. He flashed a torch into the car half-heartedly.

'Who is there?'

'Open these gates now. I don't have time for this nonsense.'

'Please, we need to know everybody who enters the house.'

70

'Whose house is it? Put Abikẹ and friend on your list and open these gates.'

'But your dad—'

'Now.'

The gates slid open and we were let in. When we drove past, I saw the guard give Abikẹ a look that I sympathised with. She must have sensed this because she said, 'Those gate men.'

'They were just doing their jobs.'

'You know, you're probably right.'

I hadn't expected her to capitulate so easily. Perhaps it was because I was in the car. At least she valued my opinion.

As we drove up to her house, I wondered what type of wealth it would take to make such an oasis, green grass watered by sprinklers while half of Lagos had no running water. We passed lush gardens that were orderly in some parts; cultivated wilderness in others. Most of the trees were full grown and a few had flowered, leaving the ground bright with petals.

When we reached Abikẹ's house, I covered a sharp intake of breath with a cough. I had seen big houses before, great colossal brutes that swallowed guests, but this thing was large in a way that did not make sense. It spread across the open space like water spilled on a smooth floor. Inside, everything was conditioned: the rugs, luxuriously soft, the air, a perfect temperature – cool enough to dry sweat, warm enough to stop my hairs from standing. It was hard not to exclaim when I saw the indoor swimming pool. It was hard but I managed to keep myself under control with a casual, 'You have a really nice place, Abike.'

After the tour, she took me to what she called her 'small' living area: a wide space with one long sofa that followed the curve of the wall. There were green plants everywhere, filling the room with a crispness that had nothing to do with the air conditioning.

'So, who else is coming?' When she'd invited me, she'd said her friends would be here. I had been in her house for an hour and still, no sign of them. Was this a date?

'Why are you asking? Are you afraid it's just going to be the two of us?'

Not afraid – glad at this second chance to talk to her alone. This time I would let her speak until I understood why she was interested in a boy who sold ice cream on the road. I hadn't always sold ice cream but she didn't know this and she had still invited me to her house. Did she think I was a charity case or—

'Don't worry, there are other people coming,' she said, bursting into my thoughts.

'That's cool.' I sounded relieved. 'Not that I would mind if it were just the two of us.'

'Well, it's not.'

Her tone was curt. Did she think I wasn't good enough to go on a date with her?

'Their names are Cynthia and Oritse. They're old friends.'

It dawned on me. She'd brought me here to amuse her friends.

72

'Do they know I'm a hawker?'

'Does it matter?'

'Do you think it matters, Abikẹ?'

If she had said no, I wonder what would have happened. She was looking at me directly, almost encouragingly as if she wouldn't have minded a hawker kissing her. But she said nothing because her friends walked in.

Cynthia was a beautiful girl, the type who is mostly eyes and who seems to flirt with everything: the walls, the sofas, me. The boy was more interesting. He was handsome but with a fleshy body that needed a few hours of hawking. Though he was impeccably dressed, his clothes were too primped to embarrass me. Once we exchanged names, he opened fire with questions.

'So what school do you go to?'

'Life Academy.'

'Sounds familiar.'

Behind me Abikẹ sniggered and I was glad we had shared this spontaneous joke.

'So how do you and Abikẹ know each other?'

I looked at her but she bent her head and studied the floor.

'We met while I was working.'

'So you work,' the girl said.

'Yes.'

'Is it in your father's company? I did that one summer. My father is an ED in Valour Bank and working with him was dull. The pay was good though. We used to cash around twenty million every . . .'

I let him run on until we were seated and a maid had brought a tray of drinks. When he stopped the girl had not forgotten.

'You still haven't told us where you work.'

Abikẹ sipped her orange juice, concentrating on the contents of her glass.

'I sell things.'

What had she told them?

'So your father owns a store and you work for him. Is that it?'

'You ask a lot of questions. Abikẹ, is this how your friends behave when they meet people?'

'Pardon them. They have no manners.'

'So, Cynthia, how do you know Abikẹ?'

The boy answered. 'We go way back. We've been in the same school for the past six years and—'

Every time I asked a question, the boy would answer. Even when I asked Abikẹ where the toilet was, he jumped in with directions.

'Go through that door and it's the first door on your left.'

'Begging should be banned in Lagos,' he said at some point in the afternoon. 'Every time you stop at a traffic light those children from Niger are there chanting, God bless you, God prosper you.'

'I still give them money, though. Don't you?'

'Of course not, Cynthia. Those people litter our streets.'

'I thought that was sweet wrappers,' I said.

'You know what I mean.'

'I don't.'

'Well, Cynthia and Abikẹ know what I mean.'

Every time his feeble opinions were challenged he re-treated to the girls. Often, Cynthia shrugged her shoulders but Abikẹ would always bounce the issue back to me.

It was only when the maid entered with the food that I got some respite. She came with a tray of scarlet *jollof* rice. The *jollof* we eat now is always a pale orange colour because tomatoes are expensive, but there in front of me was food from my childhood. I forgot Cynthia. I forgot Oritse. I even forgot Abikẹ until only a few forkfuls remained then I remembered I was not in my house. I set my fork aside and let those grains testify to the fact that I was fed at home.

Oritse sang. The timing made me uncomfortable. I was ready to leave when Abikẹ asked that he sing. Conveniently he'd brought his guitar. His voice was good, perhaps excellent, but I could not concentrate on his singing. There was something about the lyrics that made me feel like they were a secret conversation between him and Abikẹ.

He gave her pointed glances.

She pretended not to notice.

And I wondered what was going on.

All through the day I had been jangled from emotion to emotion. One minute we were sharing a private joke, the next, she was acting like she didn't know where we'd met. One minute I felt her wanting me to kiss her, the next

Oritse was singing of how he wanted to do the same. I left her house feeling tricked and manipulated. I wanted my script.

Chapter 12

When I saw my hawker this afternoon, he asked me to come to the road on Saturday.

'I can bring food and we can have a picnic in my jeep. The seats fold down.'

'No. I meant come to the road as a starting point. Your driver can drop you here then we'll go out. As in, go out into Lagos.'

'Without my driver?'

'You know, people without drivers still manage to get around.'

'And it will be just the two of us.'

'Yes.'

'What time?'

'Twelve p.m. Don't be late.'

What does someone like me wear on her first date with a hawker? One of the maids scuttled past. She looked mouldy but in her day, she would probably have been out with some hawkers. Then again, none could possibly have been like mine.

There was only one person who could advise me. In her quest to find the ultimate part, she had played love interest to a wide spectrum.

My mother was a famous actress before she met my father. According to her, when they got married, she gave up her brilliant career to be a better wife. Recognition, stringless promiscuity, they all flew out of the window to make room for her new part of loving confidante. My father did not take to the script.

Most days, you can find her wallowing in the Den, a portion of the basement that is her equivalent of the 'study'. In there, she has built a shrine to her dead career. Love Me or Die *was on when I walked in.*

'I want to ask you something.'

'Shh.'

She did not speak until her jealous co-star had strangled her to death and the credits were rolling.

'So how can I help you, Abikẹ?'

'What does one wear if one's going out with someone of a lesser social standing?'

'I presume we are speaking of a boy.'

'Yes.'

'Where is this young man taking you?'

'Not me.'

'What time of the day is this boy taking whoever we are speaking of, out?'

'In the afternoon.'

'He'll like a bit of flesh on display. That kind usually does. Is he handsome?'

'Yes.'

'Then I suggest a miniskirt: a denim one with frayed edges. Do you own anything of the sort?'

'Yes.'

'You do? I thought we weren't speaking of you. How cheap. It will suit the occasion. Is that all?'

'Yes.'

'Would you like to join me? I'm watching Best Friends Forever next. I haven't seen a movie with Jennifer and me in ages.'

'I'm busy.'

Saturday came and I was dressed in a frayed miniskirt, standing on the roadside.

On Friday evening, while Jọkẹ and I were fetching water from the communal tap, it occurred to me that Abikẹ might hate everything I'd planned.

'Jọkẹ, in five years' time when you go on your first date, where do you want to go?'

'Let me just inform you, my first date is going to be next year and the boy has to take me to a very expensive restaurant.'

'Why?'

'Because that's how a guy shows that he really likes a girl. The more expensive the restaurant the more serious the love. Don't you know?'

'I wonder who is teaching you this nonsense,' I said, heaving a twenty-litre jerry can on to my shoulder.

My sister could not be right, I thought, as I poured the water into the large drum that stood by the kitchen sink. If Abikẹ was expecting a fancy restaurant tomorrow, she might as well not leave her house. I couldn't afford the rice in the places she was used to, let alone a full meal. I had never tried to hide this.

I picked up half a tuber of yam and began to peel its skin. The mould that had eaten into it, I extracted, careful not to take off any white flesh. When we first moved here, Jọkẹ used to peel yam like we still had money. I warned her many times. Yet when I looked in the bin, I would still find peelings with shavings of white. One day, I took the knife from her and scraped the peels until they no longer had flesh on them. 'Yam is expensive in the market,' I said when I was done. Since then the shavings have been consistently brown.

I added a few stock cubes to a pot of water before setting the yam to boil. According to our roster, I cook Fridays to Sundays and Jọkẹ does the rest. Often I take some of her days during term time. I see it as an investment. It is Jọkẹ's education that will get us out of Mile 12, not my hawking and certainly not Abikẹ's money. Though my mind has wandered to some of the things she could do for us. My most extravagant dream is of moving into her house. There must be at least thirty rooms in that building. No one would notice if we took three. We wouldn't mind where she put us as long as the beds were comfortable and water came out of the taps.

After my first visit, I was bursting to describe her mansion to someone, but Aunty Precious wasn't interested and it felt wrong to tell a homeless man what I'd seen. But Mr T kept asking questions. What was her house like? How large was the garden? How many guards, did you say?

I didn't tell him we were meeting again because I didn't know if things were going to progress any further than tomorrow. No point getting excited over something that might not work out, something that perhaps I was imagining, I reminded myself, thinking of the moistness in Oritse's eyes when he looked at her.

The yam was ready.

'Jọkẹ, come and eat.'

'What did you make?'

'Mile 12 pottage.'

She lifted the lid and sniffed. 'Poor man's pottage is more accurate. There are houses in this area where they put stock fish. I know because I've eaten in them.'

'What have I told you about eating in strangers' houses?'

'They are not strangers. They are our neighbours and their *yam* pottage tastes nothing like yours. Thank you.' She took her plateful of food and flounced back to our room.

No matter what she said, this dish was not the yam pottage of my childhood. It was one born of the necessity of Mile 12 just as my culinary skills were born of my new address. In Maryland, I never even knew how to light a stove. I had to learn after we moved here, like I had to learn to chase after cars with ice cream balanced on my head.

'Mummy, food is ready.'

'Thank you.'

'Will you eat some now?'

'Later,' she said, rising and moving towards her room. 'You and Jọkẹ take your fill.'

Widowhood is not a disease, I wanted to say as I watched her shuffle to her door. Or maybe her vacancy had nothing to do with the loss of my father. Maybe she was still mourning her jewellery and manicured nails. Stripped of those things, she was nothing. She shut her door and I was left alone with my thoughts about tomorrow.

Chapter 13

'What are you wearing?'

Well I hadn't been so rude about his pink shirt.

It all started when I arrived at our meeting place and there was no hawker. Granted it would have been easier to sit in the car with the windows wound up. I had a feeling this would not fit with the day my hawker had planned.

'Hassan, disappear.'

He drove off with 2000 naira and left me glaring at anyone who wanted to grab my bag, which was everyone. I needed to relax. After all, who was going to attack me in broad daylight with at least a hundred people wandering around? My better judgement may have proved right if it were not for the outfit my mother suggested.

First, it was the drivers. Pot-bellied men leaned out of their cars to whistle at me, one fool even got out of his Peugeot to talk to me. At first I found it amusing, this sparring between myself and the randy drivers of Lagos. So far I was winning with my returns of 'Your mother' for 'Sexy lady' and 'Pervert' when an old man shouted, 'Nice legs.'

Then the pedestrians joined in. They were too close, close enough to jostle me and whisper, 'How much?' Or perhaps, if their English could not handle such complexities, 'Ashewo' would do, which though my vernacular is poor I knew meant prostitute. This too would have been all right if I'd had a chance to reply but they would walk off to be replaced by another and another before I could retort to the first. I was so busy trying to avoid these pedestrians that I didn't notice the tout until he was standing in front of me and saying, 'My name is Fire for Fire. Oya, let's go.'

Before I could decide how to respond, he grabbed my wrist. I was conscious that minimum fuss would spare me the onlookers that drift towards trouble.

'Release me,' I hissed.

'Stop pretending. You know you want do am.' He gripped me tighter and started to drag me away.

'Leave me alone,' I said more loudly now, my head turning to the passers-by.

'Help me,' I said, my free hand brushing a man balancing a load of wood on his head.

'Please.'

I saw a corn seller staring at us. She was sitting on a low stool, one rolling arm fanning the flames, her teeth running over the remains of a cob. Surely she would help me.

'Aunty,' I called out. 'Aunty, please stop him.'

'Ashewo, don't look at me.' She flung her naked cob at my feet.

Fire for Fire had not felt my nails that were clawing his arms

84

and when I kicked him he asked, 'You want make this thing painful?'

He was going to rape me, a voice murmured in my chest. He was going to take me somewhere and rape me. Abikẹ Johnson raped by a tout.

'My guy wetin you dey do with my babe?'

From behind, I heard my hawker's voice. The tout turned back and in that brief moment, I slid my hand from his grip.

'Who be you?' the tout said, reaching for me again.

'Don't try me,' my hawker said, stepping in front of me.

There was a moment I thought they would fight. Even though the tout only came up to his chest, he seemed angry enough to test his arms against my hawker's height. In the end, he settled for an empty threat. 'Me and my boys go show you.'

'Get out of here before I finish you.'

I had to save face. I delved into my little store of pidgin and called out, 'Fire for Fire don meet water.'

My indulgence drew an impersonal titter from the crowd. I looked at my hawker expectantly.

'What are you wearing?'

'What does it look like?'

A driver called out, 'Sexy lady, how much you dey charge?'

'Mind your business,' we said, momentarily on the same side.

'How can you be wearing this?'

'Did you give me a dress code?'

'You should have had the common sense to know that this,'

he said, gesturing at my legs, 'is not appropriate. You can't even go home and change because your driver has gone.'

'You should have the common sense to know that if you invite someone out, treating them like this is inappropriate. I'm going home.'

I started dialling my driver.

'No, wait. Don't do that, Abikẹ. I'm sorry.'

I kept keying in the digits.

'Please – I want you to stay.'

The phone was ringing.

'Please, just follow me home. I'll get you something to change into and we'll start again from there.'

Here was an interesting proposition. He was inviting me to his house. Even if it was only for a few minutes, it was still a breakthrough of some sort. He was beginning to trust me.

Some men were heading towards us with a man who looked like Fire for Fire at their front.

'Let's go, then.'

When we had lost the touts, we were too breathless to talk. Somewhere in our run, the tension had evaporated.

He lived in a wretched block of flats. Outside, the paint was peeling and no one had bothered to cover the cement on the inside. There was refuse everywhere. It was like the whole street was a giant dustbin. He trusted me enough to show me, something I did not take for granted, even as I stepped over a stinking gutter. His flat was not as dismal as the outside had augured. It was very dark and small, depressingly small, but everything was neatly arranged and there was no clutter.

Sitting on a chair in his living room was a woman in a pale pink dressing gown. Her eyes wandered to us and then wandered away, alighting on the all-purpose wooden table, the dwarf stove in the corner, the damp patches on the ceiling that looked like piss on white linen, before coming to rest on my face again.

'Mummy, good afternoon. This is my friend Abikẹ.'

She sat engrossed in the wall as if there were images running across it. It reminded me of my mother in the Den.

'Good afternoon.'

'Good afternoon.'

She looked like she wanted to say more but he pulled me away.

'Let's go and get the jeans.'

He led me to a door. When he opened it, his body blocked the entrance.

'What is this?'

The voice that answered his question was female. What was a girl doing in his room at this time?

'Why are you wearing—?'

I leant to the side and tried to see into the room.

'Stop!'

'I said stop!'

Pushing past him, I walked into the room. At once, everything became clear.

'Hi, my name is Abikẹ. What's yours?'

'Jọkẹ.'

From her face, that was a softer version of my hawker's, it was obvious she was his sister.

'And you?'

'Funmi.'

Under the thick powder, she might have been pretty.

'Pick the jeans so we can go. Jọkẹ, wipe that stuff off your face. I'll talk to you when I get back.'

He put a stack of trousers on the bed and left.

'I don't care what he says. I'm old enough.'

'He's your older brother,' the friend said.

'Funmi, please just continue. I don't want the eyeliner too thick.'

They spoke in low voices as if afraid I would run and tattle. I looked around the room. It was as bare as a temporary residence. There were no pictures, two lonely canisters of deodorant stood on the dressing table and a mirror reflected the blank walls. The only things of note were three checked bags shoved against a wall. I wondered what I would find if I opened one.

'You have to obey him,' the friend said, speaking louder when she saw I was ignoring them.

'Is he my father?'

'You still have to respect him.'

'I don't have to do anything!'

Her friend burst into a cackle. 'You rich people's children. Always so spoilt.'

I kept holding up a faded pair of blue jeans but I was listening now.

'Whatever. I've told you to stop talking about that.'

Like brother like sister.

'So how old are you guys?'

They turned, surprised to hear that I could speak.

'Fifteen.'

'Fourteen,' his sister said.

'That's old enough.'

'Exactly!'

When I poured the contents of my make-up bag on the bed, they moved closer but they didn't touch.

'Which eyeliner do you want? This one?'

I reached for an old pencil that I rarely used.

'Please can I have the Chanel?'

She pointed at a black and gold tube whose logo was facing down.

'How does a fourteen-year-old know about Chanel liquid eyeliner?'

I dabbed some on her upper eyelid.

'My mum used to wear it before.'

'Why only before?'

I dabbed some at the corners.

'Because she doesn't wear make-up any more.'

'How come?'

'She just doesn't.'

Like brother like sister.

*** * ***

'Which lip gloss?'
    She pointed.
    'Which eye shadow?'
    She pointed.
    'Which mascara?'

When I was done, my most expensive make-up was on her face. There was little one could add to her. She was almost a Cynthia.
    'Thank you so much.'
    Her smile was identical to my hawker's.
    'Please borrow me your eye pencil. It's better than my own.'
    I looked at the friend.
    'What you're wearing is fine.'
    'I know but my boyfriend likes it much than this and I'm going to his house now.'

As she dragged my pencil over the edges of her yellowing eyes, I wondered how I could use it again.
    'You can keep it,' I said, once she was finished.
    'Wow, thanks.'
    It would not do for his sister to dislike me after all I'd done.
    'Jọkẹ, this is for you.'

If the hawker was angry at my work, he didn't show it.
    'She's old enough to wear a little make-up,' I said and he didn't argue.

✻ ✻ ✻

She turned up in a miniskirt. Everyone knows you only wear that type of outfit in the privacy of your air-conditioned car, with the windows rolled up and preferably tinted. Everyone except Abikẹ Johnson. Flashing her legs and then wondering why a mob is chasing us.

I had to take her home. The driver had left and no self-respecting police officer would have let us walk past without stopping her for indecent dressing or worse. Still, maybe I overreacted. She was upset though she hid it well, trading insult for insult with the *danfo* drivers. I didn't know how shaken she was until she threatened to leave. Her fingers shook as she punched the numbers into her mobile phone and her eyes wouldn't meet mine. I apologised. Then, because it was the only thing to do, I offered to take her to my house to change.

With Abikẹ beside me, I felt the squalor of the place even more. The overflowing gutters, the armies of flies, the peeling paint all glared at me afresh. I almost turned back. It seemed easier to fight a hundred area boys than to let her see my apartment block.

'Don't you know the way to your house?' she said teasingly when I stopped. Really the miniskirt was not that bad. Just a little longer and it would be almost below her knees. Somebody whistled from a balcony. No. It was either she came to my flat to change or she went home.

'Don't step into the shit.'

91

When we walked in, my mother was sitting by herself in the parlour, clutching the sleeve of her nightie with one hand.

'Mummy, good afternoon. This is my friend Abikẹ.'

'Good afternoon.'

She looked blankly at us and I was afraid she would ignore Abikẹ's greeting. Finally she answered, 'Good afternoon.'

'Come,' I said, before my mother could embarrass me, 'let's go and get the jeans.'

I pushed my door open and saw Jọkẹ sitting on our bed and one of the Alabi girls drawing a line on her face.

'What is this?'

Jọkẹ turned and the Alabi girl almost poked her eye out.

'I didn't know you were coming back so early.'

'Why are you wearing make-up?'

'Funmi, you know my brother, right?'

The girl turned and I saw the rhinestones that stretched across her breasts and spelt S-E-X-Y.

'Yes. Me and your brother have met.'

'Jọkẹ, who said you can wear make-up?'

'Who said I couldn't? Funmi, please continue.'

The girl raised the pencil.

'Stop.'

'Don't listen to him.'

'I said stop!'

Abikẹ pushed into the room and stopped in the centre.

'Hi, my name is Abikẹ. What's yours?'

'Jọkẹ,' she whispered.

'And you?'

'Funmi,' the other said, her eyes focused on the floor.

I saw what Jọkẹ and the Alabi girl saw when they looked at Abikẹ, her denim so new, her bag so shiny. I understood why my sister's voice had gone quiet and the Alabi girl would not look up. I spread a pile of trousers on the bed.

'Pick a pair so we can go. Jọkẹ wipe that thing off your face. I'll talk to you when I get back.'

When she came out, Jọkẹ and the Alabi girl were following her like sheep.

'She's old enough to wear make-up,' she said as if to silence any objections I might have.

'You—'

'Just see it first.'

Jọkẹ stepped out from behind her. Apart from the shiny lips and the shimmer above her eyes, she looked no different from usual and certainly nothing like the panda next to her. Perhaps Abikẹ was right. What did I know about these things?

'Jọkẹ, let me see,' my mother said. I didn't even know she had been listening.

When she saw Jọkẹ's face, she started to cry, small tears you could flick away with your fingers, except she didn't.

'Abikẹ gave me her lip gloss,' Jọkẹ said, opening her hand to show my mother the tube. 'Can I keep it?'

'Yes,' my mother said, turning to me.

I nodded and walked to the door. 'Abikẹ, we should be leaving.'

'Is that your toilet?' she asked, pointing.

'Yes.'

It was only when she'd walked in and shut the door that I realised she wanted to use it. I waited, hoping she would work it out. It was too much to ask. First, I heard the squeaky choke of a flush button being pushed down over and over again and then finally she opened the door and pushed her head out.

'I think the toilet is broken. It's not flushing. I'm pushing down the button but no water is coming out.'

Of course nothing was coming out. Did she think water came out of the cisterns in Mile 12?

Jọkẹ answered.

'Abikẹ, we don't have running water, that's why it's not flushing. There's a bucket of water under the sink. Pour some into the bowl to flush.'

'Of course. I should have known. Thanks.'

As I heard the water slopping into the toilet, I knew she had used too much.

Chapter 14

'Welcome to Tejuosho.'

He took me down a path that kept splitting to reveal more women who were unnaturally interested in him.

'My son, come and buy from here.'

'No, I go give you beta price.'

'You know nah me get the best.'

He would nod, bow to a few, greet others. Once he said to a woman selling tomatoes, 'Mama Iyabo, wey my girlfriend?'

What?

A child crawled out from under the table and let my hawker swing her before hiding behind her mother.

'You want tomato?'

'No, I just dey show my friend around.'

I shook hands with Mama Iyabo and without knowing why, dipped my knee. She nodded with approval. I wanted to do more. Opening my bag, I began to search for my wallet.

'Bye-bye, Mama Iyabo. Make you dey look after my girl-friend.'

He took me by the elbow and moved us away.

'Why did we leave? I wanted to help that woman.'

'How nice of you. Would you buy a car just to help the seller?'

He walked a few paces before realising he was alone.

'Twice today, you have disres—'

'I'm sorry,' he said.

'Don't cut me off.'

'I'm sorry for that too.'

I let him take my hand and we entered a large warehouse crammed with even more stalls. It was dim inside. All the fluorescent lights were placed too high and many flickered on and off. I was glad that my hawker didn't have to work in a place like this.

'In a few years I want to open a stall here.'

'Why?' I asked, backing away from a skinny man who patted my arm and pointed to his table of fabric.

'I don't want to be a hawker forever. When I can afford the rent, I'm going to set up a store here and sell electronics.'

'You mean people pay rent for these spaces?'

'Of course. Every square foot is paid for. This is not a shanty market. Tejuosho is a very well-organised place.'

I looked around again. I suppose the stalls had some order. At least we could walk through them.

'So where are we going next?'

'Surulere.'

'Is it close?'

'You haven't heard of Surulere before.'

'Of course I have. I just don't know how to get there from here.'

'Are you sure you live in Lagos?'

'Shut up. How are we getting to Suruleri?'

'You mean Surulere. We're going by danfo.'

I was pressed against my hawker for most of the journey and when the danfo rattled over a pothole and flung my head against his chest, I let it lie there. Even when the conductor, a shirtless man in dirty jeans, leered and said, 'This no be hotel,' I ignored him and left my head where it was. Though the whir of the engine drowned out much, I imagined it grew easier to hear his heart beat the longer I lay pressed into him.

Lunch was served at a Mama Put. When I saw the prices chalked on the small blackboard, I almost walked out. Eating for an amount that barely classed as change scared me. My hawker was halfway through when he noticed my plate of rice was still untouched.

'Why aren't you eating?'

'Because – because I haven't washed my hands.'

'Oh sorry. I should have shown you.'

He lifted his plastic bag of drinking water and motioned for me to put out my palms. With my hands rinsed I didn't have any more excuses. I slid the spoon into the rice, wishing I'd brought my own cutlery. Who knew how many mouths had salivated over that spoon?

'Are you all right?'

'Yes,' I said, jamming the rice into my mouth. It was mushier than I would have liked and the stew was peppery but the meal was surprisingly edible.

'Aren't you going to finish your food?'

The Mama Put had been generous with her portions.

'I have.'

'Wasteful.'

'I'm not wasteful. My nannies always made me leave food on the plate.'

'My mother used to make us do the same. You would have liked her if you met her before. She had your sharp mouth.'

'Me? I'm a gentle girl.'

He pushed my shoulder, his hand lingering for longer than was necessary.

'So tell me about your own mother,' he said, leaning against the giant Iroko tree. 'What's she like?'

I hesitated.

'You don't have to tell me if you don't want to.'

I was rarely asked a question so direct. Immediately, a non-answer sprung to mind.

'She's very beautiful.'

'Like her daughter.'

I smiled at what my mother would have taken for an insult. 'No, not like me. She was a very famous actress.'

'What's her name?'

'Victoria Johnson née Ajumobi.'

'Victoria Ajumobi,' he repeated slowly.

'Have you seen Dangerous Passions, or Forbidden Fruit?'

He shook his head.

'Secret Lovers? Love me or Die?'

'Victoria Ajumobi. I'm beginning to see her face.'

'Fair, tall, slim, very large eyes.'

'Yes, of course. One of the good actresses of her generation.'

'No need to be polite. I've seen every single one of her movies and they're all crap.'

'You shouldn't say that about your mother.'

'It's true.'

'You still haven't told me anything about her.'

'I am a disappointment to her.'

'That's not true.'

'Don't pity me,' I said, turning to face him. 'I'm glad. You should have seen me when I was five. I watched all her movies, memorised the famous scenes, rehearsed their delivery . . . what a mugu.'

I shouldn't have said all this to a boy I had only known for a month. Yet he was so far outside my world. I felt safe telling him that at five, I moulded my inflections after a woman I saw more often on a screen than in real life. He would not taunt me with this image in school. He would not save it for ammunition in the next round of Frustration.

'You weren't—'

'I was pathetic,' I said, voicing a thought that had never strayed past my head. 'I was stupid to even think there was space for me in her mirror. I should have been fairer, more talented, more like her.'

He took my hand and I let him hold it, his thumb massaging my palm.

'I'm glad. I would have been a different person if she'd encouraged me. For one, I would have lived and died thinking her acting was wonderful.'

The Mama Put approached with a platter of fried meat.

'You nah don finish? You no want meat?'

The hawker shook his head yet she ladled two pieces on to his plate. 'Rice still dey for your plate. Just use this small one to finish am.'

We spent a long time under the branches of that Iroko tree. We stayed until the evening lights came on and brought the insects, until the Mama Put asked for her bench, until we could stay no longer. Once we stood, things became awkward. Behind him, I could see my car gleaming, ready to take me back.

'Thank you for a nice day.'

I wondered if he would kiss me. I knew as I lifted my face to his that I wanted him to. Abịkẹ Johnson kissing a hawker in front of a Mama Put. I didn't care who saw.

'I had a really nice time,' I said, looking directly into his eyes. Maybe he didn't like me in that way. I lowered my head, feeling foolish.

When he finally kissed me, it was a surprise. His lips rubbed mine, rough skin rubbing off my lip gloss and before I could respond, he had straightened up again.

It was a strange kiss. Not wet enough to be romantic not light enough for friends. I'm sure he will get better.

Today was her first time in Tejuosho Market. I find that incredible. Even when we lived in Maryland, we still came to

Tejuosho, though not as often as I do now. She adapted well, shaking off the hands that tried to draw her to their stalls, holding her bag tight to her body, causing drama over a small issue. Still, if you watched closely you could see she was a stranger. She didn't look at the ground when she walked and she shrank from people. Every time someone touched her or even brushed against her, she would almost recoil. Even in the *danfo* she tried not to lean against me. At first her head barely rested on my chest. As the bus moved it grew heavier until the weight was stopping me from breathing properly. I couldn't help inhaling her. She smelled of things I don't see often these days.

The Mama Put we had lunch at wasn't my usual. I was afraid we would run into one of the boys and I would have to explain myself. The food in this place isn't as good but the area is nice: a quiet side street with clean buildings that are free of listless men on their balconies. Hardly anyone used it today. There was only a dog ambling by, an old motorcycle coughing along. Every once in a while, the leaves of the Iroko tree would shiver in the breeze.

I told her about my mother to reassure us both, that once she had been different. Jọkẹ and I don't speak of her, except as one would talk of a child. Has she eaten? Has she bathed? Aunty Precious is too old for us to discuss my private life in casual conversation and Mr T is too strange. I wonder how I have survived this long without friends my age.

She told me about her mother too, an actress so famous her star did not fit in my horizon. I could not admit my ignorance without embarrassing Abikẹ. She was so certain her mother was an icon that she had built parts of herself round this fact. How could I say that her mother's name triggered no images, no films. I had to play along.

Before she left, I kissed her. While she was saying goodbye I watched her lips move. They were still glossy, even after the long day.

'I've had a really nice time.'

What would she do if I kissed her? Before I could think myself out of it, I leaned forward. She must have thought it was a hug because her arms lifted. Then she realised and dropped her hands naturally to my shoulders. My lips brushed hers. I tasted the sweet tang of apple. I was easing my mouth open when a car exhaust backfired. My head turned at the sound. We were disconnected. Her hands that lay on my shoulders now seemed to be pushing me away.

'I should go. Hassan is waiting.'

She stepped back.

'When are we seeing each other again?' I asked.

'Monday, on the road.'

She entered her car with her slim legs swaddled in my jeans. For a second, I wish I'd been foolish enough to let her walk round Lagos in a miniskirt.

Chapter 15

'When did you turn eighteen?'

'In January, before I met you.'

It had been his idea to come to the beach. Unfortunately the sun had refused to come along. The sky was grey and a cold breeze blew from the ocean. Between us lay the remains of our suya feast. The roasted meat had been too spicy at first.

'What did you do for your birthday?' I asked, sucking the last traces of pepper from my thumb.

'I went to work, came back home, had dinner and slept.'

'But it was your eighteenth. Didn't you at least have a cake?'

'No,' he said, poking the sand with a stick. 'I thought buying one was an unnecessary expense and Jọkẹ doesn't know how to bake.'

'What about your mother?'

'She used to bake before my father died. I think she's depressed now. You saw her. I wish I could buy her anti-depressants. They're too expensive. Thousands of naira for a few and once they finish what will I do?'

'I could—'

'Don't offer. Please. I'm not telling you this for charity.'

'Even if I loaned you—'

'Please, Abikẹ, drop it.'

Sometimes I admire this pride of his. Other times I think it's selfish.

'Anyway, even if she was well enough to bake, we don't have an oven. And who would I have invited to eat the cake?'

'You could have invited me.'

'I didn't know you then,' he said, scooping sand and pouring it over my toes.

'Well invite me now then.'

'I don't have any cake.'

'Just invite me.'

'OK. Will you eat birthday cake with me?'

'Yes, let's go back home. I'll bake you one.'

The kitchen keys were in the basement with Aunty Grace, my ex-nanny. We collected them from her and went back upstairs. As we entered, fluorescent lights came on, turning every surface into a mirror. I gave him the remote and began my search for ingredients.

225 grams butter.

225 grams caster sugar.

When I cracked an egg, part of the shell crumbled into the mixture.

2 tsp vanilla extract.

225 grams self-raising flour.
Heat oven to 180 °C.
Grease cake tin.
Grease baking paper.
Pour mix in.

'Done.'
  'Already?'
  'It's in the oven. I'll give it twenty minutes.'
  He switched off his episode of Fresh Prince when I sat down. A pimple had formed on my chin and all the while we spoke, I covered it with my thumb. He asked about Aunty Grace, my ex-nanny. I was fond of her once. He told me about his father. An accident killed him. I was about to ask what his job had been, when I smelt smoke.
  'The cake!'
  When I brought it out, the top was an even black.
  'I'll get Hassan to buy something from close by.'
  'What's wrong with this one?'
  'It's burnt.'
  'It's only the top that's burnt. We can manage it.'
  'You can't have burnt cake for your eighteenth birthday.'
  'I was actually hoping you wouldn't take it out when it was nice and golden-brown.'

  He ate it. I couldn't take more than a bite of my slice but he finished his and asked for more. It was as I watched him bravely demolishing his second portion that I thought maybe what I felt for him was love. Not the stuff my mother overacted on screen. It was quiet but confident. He looked up while I was studying him. A cake crumb marred his left cheek. As I brushed it away, he took my palm and kissed it. I felt him ready to say what had been passing through my mind.

'Abikẹ, Aunty Grace said I should check if you have finished so I can come and clean up.'

I turned and glared at the maid. It was only my hawker's presence that stopped me from saying more than, 'Thank you. We'll be done later.'

When she left I turned back to my hawker. The moment was gone.

'I should be going, Abikẹ. It's getting late but thank you so much for this.'

'Wait. I—' My training has made me a coward in such matters. 'I want to make a party pack for you.'

'Oh.'

'Yes. The celebrant can't leave without a party pack.'

For a few moments after he left, I remained in the kitchen, watching the maid clean up. She was very conscientious, wiping everything twice before putting it away. It was because I was there.

'Take this key and lock up when you finish.'

'Aunty Grace said I should tell you to bring it. She wants to talk to you.'

I did not want to talk to her. She was always trying to remake the time when she had been like my mother. I don't remember when I started noticing that she had no style and her

English was as simple as a child's. Once I saw, there was no go-
ing back.

'Just take it to her. I have some homework to do.'

I chose the beach because it was a setting more obviously romantic than her parlour or the Mama Put near my house. I
chose wrongly. It would have been better to stay in Mile 12.
The beach was crowded with beggars and white-garmented
church members. The water was too cold for wading and
the sand was damp. I thought she just wanted to leave when
she offered to bake me a birthday cake. When we got to her
house, instead of going to her living room as I had expected, we descended a flight of stairs. After one floor, we stood
at the start of a starkly lit corridor that stretched past many
doors.

'Where are we?'

'Boys' quarters. Most of the unmarried servants live here.
The left half is for men. The right is for women.'

As we walked, I peeped into the lives of these downstairs
people. Their rooms were pristine, each one a replica of the
last, each occupant dressed in identical uniform. Many came
out to greet her. Finally she stopped at a door and knocked.

'It's Abike.'

The door opened and a squat beaming woman stood on
the threshold.

'Abike, long time. You don't come and visit me again.
Who is this handsome boy? Is he your boyfriend?'

She ignored the question.

'Good afternoon, Aunty Grace. Please can I have the key

to the kitchen?'

'What do you want to eat? I'll send somebody to make it for you.'

'Don't worry; I'll do it myself. Thank you.'

Her voice was tender and she called this maid, who could be no relative of hers, Aunty.

'Here is the key. When you finish bring it so we can talk. I've missed you.'

My mother would have loved the kitchen. It seemed new. The granite floors shone almost as brightly as the lights they reflected. There was a small TV in the corner. While she baked, I watched an episode of what used to be a favourite show. It had been long since I had sat in front of a television by myself. I had lost the habit. I was glad when she put the cake in the oven and came to sit next to me. I switched off the TV.

'Don't let me interrupt.'

'No, let's talk instead. Tell me about Aunty Grace. The two of you seem very close.'

'We used to be when I was younger. Typical story. The maid changed my nappies, carried me when I cried, was the last person I saw before I went to sleep . . . There's one point I thought she was my real mother and my father refused to marry her because she wasn't beautiful. Then I grew up and became more interested in spending time with people my own age. Also, my father said it wasn't proper for me to be so close to a maid.'

'I wonder what he would think of me.'

'He doesn't approve of any guy I know. What about you? Did you have a maid that you were very attached to?'

'I'm a hawker. What do you think?'

I wasn't ready to tell her how much my life had changed. What if she didn't believe me? That would hurt more than her thinking I was born with no wider prospects than running on the road.

'How did your father die?'

'In a car accident.'

I remember the day we found out. My mother took me to identify the body. At the last moment she changed her mind, leaving me standing in the waiting room too disgusted by the stained chairs to sit. I knew the body would not be his. We would drive home and my father would be sitting in the living room reading a newspaper. Instead, when she came out, she had aged in expression. She hugged me and I inhaled the faint smell of smoke and meat that had not been on her clothes before.

'If he had been sick, at least we would have been able to prepare but it was so sudden. He didn't come back from work on Friday. On Saturday we got a phone call saying he was dead. I was man of the house at fifteen. My mother was better then. Still I had to remind her to eat sometimes. One day I found Jọkẹ, leaning against the wall, crying. I wanted to join her but I had to be strong. I was the tissue bringer.'

She reached across the table and touched my hand.

'What wor—'

'I think something is burning.'

***

It was the cake. I didn't mind it being burnt. Just the offer would have been enough for me.

'Abikẹ, it's really nice.'

'I'm the one that made it and I can't even lie to myself.'

While she wasn't looking, I sneaked some eggshell out of my mouth.

'Don't disagree with the celebrant. I like the cake.'

'The celebrant has some cake on his face.'

'Where?' I asked, raising my hand to my left cheek.

'To the left.'

I moved my hand.

'*Your* left.'

I deliberately placed my hand further away from the crumb.

'Don't worry. I'll do it.'

She reached across to brush my face and was about to withdraw when I took her hand. I kissed it in the place her palm joined with her wrist.

'Abikẹ—'

Her maid walked in, breaking the moment. I thought she would say something when the maid had left. Instead she offered to make me a party pack.

'Abikẹ, this is too much. Just a slice of cake would be fine.'

'No, take it. It's the least I can do after making you eat burnt food.'

'Thank you. Jọkẹ and my mother will enjoy this.'

'And you too. It's for you as well.'

Jọkẹ was sitting at the table doing her homework when I got home.

'What's this?'

'Look and see.'

By the time she'd got to the bottom of the bag, I had to tell her to be quiet, afraid the neighbours would complain.

'Who gave you?'

'Abikẹ. She came to the house the other day.'

'Is she your girlfriend?'

'No, she's not.'

'Then why would she give you all this?' Before I could answer, Jọkẹ had taken the bag to my mother's room. 'Mummy, look. Toblerone. Grapes. Apples.'

I was relieved when the maid interrupted us today. If she hadn't, I would have asked Abikẹ to be my girlfriend and I might be sitting at home now, nursing a rejection. It is pleasanter to live in this precarious hope than to know for certain she doesn't want me.

Chapter 16

I don't know where going to Yale will leave my hawker and me.
A long-distance relationship is impossible with someone who
doesn't have a phone and will never let me buy him one. I could
fly down every holiday but that would still leave months where
we wouldn't have contact with each other. What am I worrying about? Are we even in a relationship? He's kissed me once
on the palm and once on my lips. That may mean nothing to
him. I've done as much with Oritse in a school dance and we've
never moved further than flirting.

Last week he came to my house to watch a rom-com I hoped
would spur him on. Throughout the movie, he held my hand,
sometimes rubbing his thumb over my palm. Apart from this
light teasing, he ignored the excellent example of the lead actor
and neither strayed past my hands nor made any bold declara-
tions.

I gave him a bottle of shower gel Cynthia had wrapped because he'd mentioned Jọkẹ didn't like the soap he bought. He
refused to take it until he knew what was inside and he refused
to take it when I told him.

'When it finishes?'

'I'll give her another one.'

He shook his head. 'We can't keep borrowing soap from you, Abikẹ.'

'It's a gift.'

'You know I can't accept it.'

It was true. I knew he wouldn't accept it though he has never told me why. The label 'used to be rich' hangs from everything that concerns him. Yet, he will not tell me how he ended up a hawker. I'm almost certain his father's death was the key. There's nothing new in that. Every year or so someone drops out of Forest House because their father has died and they can't afford the fees any more. They may not become hawkers but some find their position drastically altered. I just wish he'd trust me enough to tell me that once he was more than a hawker and his father's death changed all that.

I wish Abikẹ would be like my mother and be more forthcoming. My father was the son of a peasant farmer from Ondo State. My mother was the daughter of an Igbo car magnate. As she often recounted proudly, she had been the instigator.

'I knew your father liked me,' she would say, speaking to us but looking at him. 'He was very shy and I was a babe on campus. He was always staring at me but whenever I looked his way, he would pretend he could not see me. So one day I walked up to him and said, "Is there something on my face."'

Here, always, he would interrupt, leaning forward in his

leather armchair. 'No, children. Don't listen to your mother. What she said was, "Is there something *wrong* with my face? And I said—"

'Then your father said, "No. Far from it. Your face is the most beautiful face I have ever seen." Your dad knew how to toast a girl.'

Except, of course, she was the one who did all the toasting. When my grandfather threatened to disown her if she brought Yoruba labourers into his family, my father, ever timid, considered ending their relationship.

'Girls from good homes didn't marry without their parents' permission,' he would explain sheepishly when they reached this point.

'Yes but your grandfather was a tribalist. That was the only reason he refused to let me and your father marry. Tribalism is what is holding Nigeria back. You must never judge someone based on their tribe.'

We would nod absently. Jọkẹ's Barbie and my Gameboy always more interesting than the tired story of how my parents got married.

If anyone could teach me how to toast Abikẹ it would be my mother. Only she could explain the inner workings of a girl who has always had everything. Which words would I use to start such a conversation? Mother, I think I am in love with a girl. Mum, I know I am in love. Mummy, please help me to toast this girl.

Maybe it is normal for Abikẹ to kiss boys. Maybe this means nothing to her. Without a clear sign, I do not know how to trick myself into believing I am enough. Yet, she is different enough for me to try. She is not like the friends who disappeared soon after my private school 'excluded' us for not being able to pay the fees. They were happy to come to Maryland and offer their consolations. Once we moved to Mile 12 it was a different story. The first time Tunde came to the flat, I opened the door and found him covering his nose.

'My guy, how do you deal with the stench? Let's go out, please.'

His driver took us to the cinema. At the front of the queue, I found out ticket prices had increased.

'No problem, it's just a hundred naira you need,' he said, sliding the money out of his stuffed wallet.

The following weekend, once I opened the door and saw him standing with his hand over his nose I said, 'Let's do something in the area.'

'There's a party—'

'No. I don't want to go for any party. I just want to chill. The Mama Put down the road serves really good food.'

He winced when I said Mama Put.

'Or we can eat here.'

'No. Thanks. I'm not hungry.'

'Since when? You're always hungry.'

'There will be food at the party.'

'There's food here.'

'Bros, don't be offended. My mum said I shouldn't eat anything here. Let's just go to the party.'

It was something my mother would have said when we

lived in Maryland and could afford such snobberies.

'I don't want to go to the party.'

If things were reversed and Tunde was the one in Mile 12, I would have ignored my mother.

'OK, see you soon then.'

That was the last time I saw him or anyone else from my school.

Abikẹ is as comfortable in her mansion as she is in a Mama Put. I've told her of how Jọkẹ wants to be an engineer. I've told her of the first time I chased after a *danfo* bus. I've even told her of how I felt after my father's accident, something I've never mentioned to my mother. My story is my only thing of value so I am sparing with it.

Nothing has happened since the day I kissed her palm. On days when the sun has made me delirious, I imagine she is in love with me. On other days when the rain has turned me cold, I know this is just an experiment. Yet I still hope. Whenever she takes my hand, or laughs at something I have said, despite myself, this deluded feeling flares up and threatens to drive away all common sense.

The first girl I ever told 'I love you' was Ego Ofili. We were fourteen, in the same class. Many seniors wanted her chest that was more than twice her age but I did not want Ego just for her stupendous 32J breasts, according to toilet rumours. I also wanted her because when we were paired on a school trip, I discovered that a girl could be more than her bra size. Ego was funny, she laughed confidently, she had opinions on football yet she could still make me feel breathless when her fingers brushed against my arm.

'I love you,' I said into her ear one day, after weeks of gathering courage. I waited for the effect my words would have.

None, it turned out, and I have never had occasion to repeat them. I don't find any of the Mile 12 girls attractive. It is Abikẹ that I want as a girlfriend. I will tell her soon.

Chapter 17

*All bad things come to an end is a more comforting maxim
than the other one.*

The first thing my father said, after he had kissed me and
gone through a list of pleasantries, was, 'Abikẹ, I have warned
you about bringing strangers into my house.'

And the next round began.

'Who?'

'Your new hawker friend.'

'He's not a stranger. You know of him.'

'"And friend" was the entry in the logbook. I do not want
any "and friends" in my house.'

'So you want to know his name?'

'I will not have boys you picked off the street in my house.'

'Where do you think I picked Oritse and Cynthia from?'

The tips of his fingers touched as he studied my face.

'I see. So you have introduced this boy into the group to an-
tagonise the rest. A friendship with a hawker to make them
unsure of their position.'

I said nothing.

'When am I going to meet this boy?'

'Whenever. He's here a lot. '

'Next Wednesday.'

'He works on weekdays.'

'And I'm not here on weekends.'

Offer him something.

'You should see what we do when you're not around.'

He said nothing.

'You can meet him if you are so desperate.'

Silence.

'I'll throw a party. I'll make sure he doesn't leave till he's seen you. Are you happy?'

'Write his name next time.'

I was in Cynthia's car, thankful that she had seen me walking down the driveway and offered me a lift. The day had been spent sparring with Oritse and two replicas of him. I'd been hoping that Abikẹ and I would get a few minutes alone so I could say the I-love-you I'd been practising. The seconds never materialised. Ikenna and Chike were even worse than Oritse when it came to pushing their way into side conversations. In a brief moment I'd had, while the rest were discussing school, I asked if we would be alone the next time I came. She said yes.

'How come your driver doesn't come to pick you?'

'Pardon?' I'd forgotten Cynthia was in the car.

'Why doesn't your driver pick you?'

So Abikẹ had really not told them anything about me.

'Taking public transport means I'm independent.' It was close to the truth.

'Your parents could get you a car.'

'I want to buy one with my own money.'

'Oh yes. You said. You work in your father's business.'

What would she do if she found out I was a hawker? I didn't care. It made no difference what Cynthia thought of me.

'So what do you think of Abikẹ?'

'I really like her. She's a very nice girl.'

'What do you think of me?' I glanced at her. I couldn't see her face because she was staring into the growing darkness, the absence of street lighting emphasising the murkiness of everything that lay outside.

'Well, I think you're a nice girl too.'

'Ha! More like you think I'm very boring. Abikẹ's bland sidekick. The beautiful girl that ornaments the room.'

'No. Not at all.'

'Whatever. You wouldn't be the first. Do you know why I became friends with her? My father was in trouble at work. He works for her father. I become her friend, get into the elite circle that grovels around her and suddenly Popsy is coming in for a promotion.'

'Oh.'

'Do you know why I'm so boring?'

'No. I mean you're not – I don't think—'

'It's because Abikẹ likes me this way. She's not going to have competition. She'll let me in because I'm pretty but I'd better not use that against her. So I sit there and sigh or else maybe Popsy might be getting a letter from the boss.'

It all seemed a little far-fetched. This powerful business-man handing out promotions at the whim of a teenager.

'What do you think of Oritse? You don't want to know? She's caught you, hasn't she?'

'No one has caught me.'

'You think Oritse likes her, don't you? Well, he doesn't.'

'How do you know?'

'Because we're going out.'

I had misread things. Abikẹ and Oritse were friends. There was no one in my way.

Surely there was something I was forgetting.

'What about the song?'

'Abikẹ's father is on the board of one of the leading record labels in this country. You've heard Oritse sing. All he needs is someone like Mr Johnson to take an interest in him. Till that happens, he'll keep writing songs that are supposedly about Abikẹ.'

'So you're using Abikẹ for what her father can give you.'

'Spare your pity. She's the one that wants to have the tal-ented, the beautiful, the cleverest running around to her orders.'

'Why are you telling me all this?'

'We thought you would ask. Out of all of us that are in "the group", you're the only one that has nothing to lose by making Abikẹ feel sorry. Or is there something you want from Mr Johnson?'

'Why would I want to make Abikẹ feel sorry?'

'It's early days. You'll soon find out. Which turning do we

take?'

'Don't worry, I'll get down here.'

The car stopped and I stepped into one of the suburbs that preceded Mile 12.

'Think about it,' she said. 'Watch her. You'll see.'

Chapter 18

'Abikẹ, what does your father do?'

'Many things.'

'Like what?'

'Shipping, construction, insurance, electronics. Olumide Johnson does everything. Why?'

'I was just wondering what it took to build a house like yours.'

'Very funny.'

We were in the pool but we weren't swimming. What he loved was the simulated waves drifting him wherever they pleased. Sometimes our bodies would bump against each other. While we were floating, one of my half-brothers walked in with a towel draped round his neck. Once he saw me, he turned and left.

'Who was that?'

Before my parents got married, my father was a notorious bachelor. According to him, people said that he only had to glance at a woman for her to feel a kick in her stomach. My half-siblings are the remains of all that excitement. As I live in an opposite wing of the house, I never see them. Sometimes my father tells me snippets of their stories. A few years ago, he threw out all the girls when rumours of half-incest began to cling around the eldest boy.

I considered lying. What did I have to hide? 'It was my half-brother.'
    'You never told me you had siblings.'
    'Half.'
    'How many half-siblings do you have?'
    The truth was I didn't know.
    'Nine.' It seemed a plausible number.
    'Where do they all live?'
    'On the other side of the house.'
    'How come I've never met them?'
    'They're all older than me. Busy schedules.'
    'Oh.'

The next time we touched: 'Why are you friends with Oritse?' He sounded jealous.
    'Why do you ask?'
    'I don't know. The two of you don't seem very alike.'
    'We're not. I just enjoy his company.'
    'Does his voice have anything to do with it?' He sounded up-set.
    'I guess so. We both love music but that's all we are: friends.'
    'Mm.'
    His fingers brushed my thigh but he withdrew.

'I should go.'

I watched the water run down his chest as he climbed out of the pool. Last weekend he had asked if we would be alone. It had made me certain he would say something today. Let him take his time. It can't be far. Why else would he be jealous of Oritse?

'I'll see myself out since you're too lazy to move.'

'Don't forget I still have one more week of Easter holiday. I won't see you on the road this week.'

'See you next weekend then. Here or the road?'

It was easier to have privacy in my house.

'Here. See you Saturday. Twelve o'clock.'

The water lapped over his handprints and I closed my eyes.

She remained floating in the pool, long after she thought I'd left. Her hair trailed like a wet mop. Her eyes were closed, leaving her face a mask. As I towelled myself dry I wondered about that half-brother. What was to stop me from wandering to the other side of the house and bumping into him or another one of her half-siblings?

Getting to the other side of the house proved difficult. Corridors ran into staircases that led to unused living rooms. Eventually, I began to feel like I was moving through the place. The furniture changed. The tasteful opulence faded into bright orange chairs that didn't smell new. In Abikẹ's quarters you only heard the purring of air conditioners. Now I could hear speech, fragments of sentences that came from nowhere. I saw my first human being halfway down a corridor: a maid.

'Excuse me, are you looking for something?'

I turned to face her: a short woman whose discoloured

skin spoke of many years of bleaching.

'Yes. I'm here to visit one of Oga's children.'

'Which one?'

'Junior.' Every family had a Junior.

'Junior? Are you talking about Wale?'

'Yes, some people call him that.'

'Go straight. Take the second door for your right and the third door for your left. You want me to show you?'

'No. I'll be fine.'

Second right, third left, knock.

'Come in.'

It was him. The towel was still draped around his shoulder, the swimming shorts still on.

'Who are you?' The voice was low and masculine. It was odd coming from a face that mirrored Abikẹ's so closely.

'Are you Wale?'

'Yes.'

His short answer flustered me into an unplanned lie.

'Abikẹ asked me to tell you that the pool is free.'

I noticed the angular pistol that lay quietly in his lap.

'You're lying,' he said, tracing the muzzle. 'Because Abikẹ doesn't even know my name and even if she did, such a message is not her style.'

In one movement the gun left his lap and was staring into the space between my eyes.

'So tell me your name and tell me the real reason why you are here.'

It seemed preposterous that this boy would shoot me in the

afternoon in a house full of people. I could have turned and walked away but as I watched his index finger flex round the trigger, I felt my spine itch where the bullet would shatter it.

I told him my middle name.

'Sit down. You're making me uncomfortable.'

Behind me the door was still open. I could rush out and not slow down until I had passed the maid, passed the cheap orange chairs, passed the third empty corridor and I was in Abikẹ's side of the house again.

'Please sit down,' he said waving the gun as I leant back into the empty doorway.

'Why won't he sit down?' he muttered to himself. He gave a short laugh and threw the gun under the bed.

'Don't mind me, jo. The thing isn't even loaded. I just like to pretend sometimes. Seriously, I'm sorry. I was just joking with the stupid thing. Please sit down.' His voice was thinner now, creeping into a whine.

'Thank you,' he said when I sat. 'So what do you want to know since we have established that Abikẹ didn't send you?'

'She—'

'Shut up.'

'Pardon?'

'I mean please be quiet. I'm trying to find out who you are. You must be friends because you were in the pool together. Or are you more than friends? The princess's consort, her toy boy?'

'Watch your mouth.'

'I'm just throwing out possibilities. You saw me walk in. She didn't send you to me. You came looking for me. Why?

127

Why have you come to look for me?'

Can you tell me who Abikẹ is?

The question sounded naive in my head. Instead of matching his directness I found myself saying, 'I was curious to see what Abikẹ's brother would be like.'

'Half-brother,' said the spitting image of Abikẹ. 'Half.'

'She's never mentioned you before. I was curious.'

'She's never mentioned me before, you were suspicious. So you want my story. No, don't be silly. You don't want my story. You want my story to tell you things about Abikẹ you don't know. Why? Why would my coming in make you suspicious? It wouldn't. Some people just don't like their half-siblings. It wouldn't unless you were suspicious already. What are you suspicious of?'

'Tell me.'

'You're scared something you heard about her is true.'

'Not scared.'

'Angry, upset, scared, whatever.' The possibilities floated up to the ceiling. 'Who did you hear it from? No, don't tell me. It doesn't matter because I know what they said.'

'How?'

'Because she is just like her father, a cruel, conniving son of a bitch.'

The words were too harsh. At worst, Cynthia had called her manipulative.

'You don't believe me?'

I could have left then. I might not know Abikẹ but neither did this boy.

'Follow me.'

Chapter 19

I remained in the pool long after my hawker left, floating on my back and staring at the ceiling. I haven't told him about the party yet. What if my father hates him when they meet or, even worse, what if they click? If my father forbade me from seeing him, I wouldn't think twice about disobeying, but what if he approves. What if Olumide Kayode Johnson approves of my taste in boys?

If I don't throw this party, my father will wonder why this hawker is too special to be seen. The last thing I want is him thinking my hawker is special. He couldn't run him over – my hawker is not a dog to be crushed by the tyres of his Jaguar – but he would find a way to twist everything I know about my hawker into a lie.

He did it with this boy I was seeing before, Michael. He was nineteen at the time, five years older than me. Fuzz grew on his chin where the boys in my class were battling pimples. He had crossed into the exotic world of higher education. Although higher education in Ghana. Of course I couldn't hide him for long.

'Abikẹ, who is this boy I'm hearing about?' my father asked one Wednesday.

'I know many boys.'

'You know who I'm talking about. Look at me. Michael Effiong, that's his name, isn't it? I hope you know he's only using you to get to me.'

'That's very flattering. Michael does not even know who you are.'

'Am I the one doing the flattering? What do you think he sees in you? He's older and from what I hear he's good-looking too.'

'And from what I hear, I thought you had better things to do.'

I won that night. The next Wednesday when I walked into his office, Mr Dosunmu was standing next to him instead of outside by the door.

'Dosunmu, call him.'

The stooge bowed and put the phone on speaker. As it rang my father and I stared at each other, his passive expression mirroring mine.

'Hello.'

I opened my mouth. My father's hand silenced me.

'Hello,' Michael said again, his voice as usual, manlier and deeper on the phone.

Mr Dosunmu looked at my father who looked at me. I nodded and relaxed into my chair. Whatever the test, Michael would pass.

'Hello, good evening,' Mr Dosunmu said in his soft voice. 'Is *this Mr Michael Effiong?'*

'Yes: who is this?'

'Charles Dosunmu calling from Johnson Petroleum about your application.'

On the other end, Michael inhaled deeply. When he spoke, his voice had climbed a few notes. 'Good evening, sir. I'm so glad to receive this call. I thought I had been rejected since so many weeks had passed.'

'My boss and I were impressed by your CV. Not many university students start looking so early so we would like to offer you a job in our engineering department during this year's long vacation.'

Michael inhaled again. 'Thank you very much, sir. I am so grateful.'

'We will send you further details via email. Is there any message you want me to pass across to my boss?'

'You mean Mr Johnson himself?'

'Yes, Mr Effiong.'

'Please tell him,' he paused to gather himself. 'Please tell him that I am so thankful and I will do my best to prove myself worthy of this opportunity.'

'That's very good, Mr Effiong. My boss has a message for you as well. He wants you to know that your connection to his daughter had nothing to do with the offer.'

It was his cue for shock. To think Abikẹ Johnson was the same Johnson as Olumide. To think he had been seeing me when he sent his CV to my father's company. All Michael said was, 'Yes, sir. Of course, sir.'

It proved nothing. After all Michael had never told me to

put in a good word but how long would he have waited before asking? Two months after his CV had gone unanswered? Three?

My hawker is not a Michael. If he were ever to use me, it would not be because my father is Olumide Johnson but because my father is a rich man. This I can forgive. He would not be a human being if my black jeep had not made me more attractive; if my large house had not added to my cachet. Were my father to trick him into revealing this, it would not change anything. I know there is more to us than my jeep or my house.

'Where are we going?'

He was leading me down another corridor. I was finding it hard to keep up with his long strides.

'Why are we walking so fast?'

He didn't answer. I followed him down a flight of stairs. Then a corridor. Then up another flight of stairs. Breathless and annoyed, I grabbed one of his arms as it swung behind him.

'Can you just tell me where we're going?'

'You're the one who wants to find out something, so shut up and follow me.'

He continued striding down the corridor.

'Don't speak to me like that.'

'Shh.'

'Don't shush me.'

He ran back and pushed my shoulder roughly. 'Be quiet. He doesn't like noise in his part of the house.' I had made a crack in that calm exterior. Was that fear I saw in his eyes?

A door opened and a shape stepped out, blocking the light coming from the other end of the corridor.

'How many times have I told you to be quiet when you're walking through my house?'

At worst the voice was mildly irate.

'I'm sorry,' Wale called out, clutching the hem of his shirt.

'Who is that?'

The shape flicked a switch and flooded the corridor with light. It was a man. A dark man in a black suit.

'Come here.'

We walked towards the shape.

'So, Wale, it's you.'

From behind me Wale answered, 'Yes, sir.'

'I'm sorry, sir. It was my fault. I was the one making noise.'

He peered down at me, a birthmark on his temple and a small frown the only things that marred his handsome features.

'And who are you?'

'I'm Ab—'

'He's my friend.'

'Well, tell your friend not to speak when I have the intention of speaking.'

'He's sorry.'

'You can't even take responsibility for your own actions. Looking at you, I may have to ask Dosunmu to arrange another test. The results of the last one were inconclusive.'

What was he talking about and why had Wale shrunk when he said test?

He turned and walked away. We watched his diminishing figure, the close-fitting suit, the knock, knock, knocking of footsteps meeting hard wooden floor. Long after the sound had died we remained in the corridor, lost in our heads.

So her father was a bully. I hadn't expected more from a man who could build such a house but I had hoped he would be different. I'd dreamt that when we met and Abikẹ told him I was a hawker, he would understand that people could climb up. Instead, here was my parents' story all over again. If one day Abikẹ had to choose, would I be enough?

Beside me, Wale was leaning against the wall, covering his eyes with his hands.

'He's probably just busy,' I said.

'You don't understand.'

'I'll understand if you want me to leave.'

'No. Follow me,' he said for the second time, but now his gait was tired. As we shuffled towards the end of the corridor, it occurred to me that Abikẹ's part of the house was not that different from this section. No, it wasn't that different at all.

Chapter 20

While I was rubbing in cream, I wondered if I should call my party planner, to see if she had come up with any ideas for a theme. She hadn't been my first choice. Yesterday I went to her agency to ask for my usual. She was booked.

'Are you sure?'

'Yes, ma,' the receptionist said, reading off her screen.

'Let me speak to your manager.'

She came out of her office, she remarked on how lovely it was to see me and how lovely I looked and how lovely everything was but I could not have Deji.

'What about Tope?'

'I'm sorry, Tope is booked.'

'For what?'

'A wedding.'

Tayo, Derin, Buki, they were all booked.

'Even for a customer like myself?'

'Abikę, I'm sorry. It's wedding season. I would if I could but they're all so close to the date and this new secretary forgot to leave someone free for your family.'

The woman behind the desk lowered her head at this hastily concocted lie.

'If you don't have someone, I'll go somewhere else.'

'Oh no, I didn't say that. I just said we don't have any of the girls you asked for. There's this new girl, Nkem. She's wonderful.'

'Nkem?'

'Yes, a lovely Igbo girl. What date do you want her for?'

'Let me see her first.'

Tribe doesn't matter any more. Everyone still knows that the Igbos don't have style.

'Didn't you hear the customer? Go and get me Nkem.' The receptionist stumbled out of her seat and disappeared into a back room.

I heard her clicking heels before I saw her. She was light-skinned, tall, noticeable if not pretty.

'Yes, madam, you called me.'

Her voice was deep and her speech clipped, almost British. Not quite.

'I wanted to introduce you to your new customer.'

Nkem gave me a pageant smile, widening her eyes and lowering her head. 'Nkem Ejike,' she said, advancing with an outstretched hand. Even her name was mutilated by that strange accent of hers. I nodded at the manager. It would be a shame to fail her after all that effort.

So far she hasn't disappointed. She remembered the weekend I had in mind clashed with a big concert. On the question of venue, we have decided to use my house. This means that my father will definitely attend. Time remains unsettled. Though afternoon parties are generally for children, there is an appealing straightforwardness to them. Once the sun sets on an event, make-up thickens and voices mysteriously deepen. Yet for all the falseness of evening parties, their effect is longer lasting.

Of course these are just preliminaries. As Nkem takes notes on diamanté-free stationery, there is hope.

Wale and I walked through a large wooden door into a room that was barely cooled by the rusty fans circling over our heads. It was the first room I had seen in this house that was almost the same temperature as the rest of Lagos. The second thing that struck me, even more powerfully, was that every single person in the room was male.

'Are these your brothers?'

'Yes they are.'

'All of them?'

'Half-brothers.'

There was a boy so dark his white teeth looked fake. On the far side of the room, a scrawny boy was playing table tennis with the wall, his face a bleached yellow, his fair skin bursting with strawberry pimples.

'You guys, this is my friend.' The small clutch gathered round the television grunted their hellos at me. It was strange, all these boys, some of them older than me, watching TV on a Saturday afternoon.

'Don't mind them. They're usually more polite. This is

what TV does.' We moved through the room, an introduction here, a smile there. 'You should probably meet Chief.'

'Who?'

'He's the oldest of us all. Twenty-eight next year.'

He led me to a side table where a hulk with excessive facial hair was playing Ludo with a boy of about fifteen.

'My brother.'

I put out my hand but he just stared at it, hissing.

'Don't do that,' the fifteen-year-old said from behind me, 'He doesn't like people disturbing his Ludo.'

'*This* is my eldest brother.' Wale said. I turned to face the boy with no facial hair and with skin as smooth as a small boy's.

'I'm sorry. I—'

'There's no need. It's not the first time such a thing has happened. I can assure, it won't be the last.'

'Chief, my friend here, who is also Abikẹ's friend, wants to find out about her.'

'Why?'

'He's suspicious.'

'Well, we won't be very useful. We don't know her very well.'

'How come? Aren't you all siblings?' I said before Wale could interrupt again.

'Half-siblings. Sit down.'

I sat and Wale stood behind me, his arm draped on the back of my chair.

'So, what do you want to know about Abikẹ?'

'What do you think of her?'

'I know very little of her. She lives in her section. We live in ours. We've been ordered not to go to that part and she's shown no interest in us. Look at him.' I glanced at the hulk still rolling the dice and counting the squares, not realising his opponent had left. 'He had a breakdown a few months ago. No one is sure why. She must have heard but she never came.'

'She might have a good reason,' I said, rushing to her defence and instantly feeling less guilty about being there.

'Yes. Maybe,' Chief said, tapping his fingers on the glass screen of the Ludo board. 'Is there anything else you want to know?'

I looked round the overwhelmingly masculine room. 'How come you don't have any sisters?'

'We do.'

'Where are they?'

'A few years ago, our father decided to send them all away.'

'Why?'

'Because he can. Of course he didn't send Abikẹ away and of course, she did nothing to stop him.'

'It is not her fault that she is the favourite child,' I said, raising my voice above Chief's conspiratorial whisper.

He looked at me pityingly. 'How do you think she became his favourite child? There was a time when we all lived together. We all had access to my father. We were all his children. Now she has poisoned his mind against us. She is the reason our living room looks like this; why none of us went to university abroad, why our father is one of the richest men in Africa and we have not seen one kobo.'

'It could have been her mother that turned him against you.'

He shook his head. 'You cannot blame her mother. If you'd met her you would see that she is as much a victim as the rest of us. No. Abikẹ did it by herself. She is his daughter.'

'Aren't you all his sons?'

'Yes we are his sons, we have taken three DNA tests to prove.'

So that was the test Mr Johnson had mentioned in the corridor. No wonder it had shaken Wale so badly. What kind of father would put his children through such an ordeal?

'What about Abikẹ? Did she have to take any tests?'

'Of course not. Abikẹ is special. She is like him.'

'What do you mean?'

He caught Wale's eye. 'This boy does not know our father.' He looked at me again. 'You don't know what type of man Olumide Kayode Johnson is?'

When I shook my head his face froze in irritation.

'Wale, why have you brought me this small boy?'

He dropped the insult carelessly without meeting my eye. Wale's hand fell on my shoulder. 'It's time to go.'

'Wait,' I said, shrugging him off. 'How many half-siblings do you have?'

'Thirteen,' he answered before giving a small cough. 'I must leave you with Wale now. I'm keeping my brother waiting.'

'So what do you think?' Wale asked as we left the room.

'Of what?'

'Chief.'

'I don't know. He seemed all right.'

'He's better than all right. He's the only one brave enough to stand up to our father. If not for him, we would be cut out of—'

'Cut out of what?'

He shook his head and an echo of Chief's irritated look settled on his face.

'Don't worry about that. Just walk down these stairs and take the door in front of you to get out.'

'Thanks.'

'Keep your eyes open. You'll see we're telling the truth,' he said, turning to make his way back to his brothers.

Chapter 21

Nkem would not be amused if she found out her carefully planned party was centred on the preferences of a street hawker. It is a gesture he will probably never fully appreciate. I can't spend the whole evening pointing out 'Nasco Love' keeps playing and my dress is the same shade as his bright pink shirt. In a way, the party has nothing to do with him. For once, I feel like doing something completely outside Frustration. Just to see.

I know he won't take advantage of me if he realises how much I am willing to spend on him. I know he won't stop talking to me if the party somehow contrives to flop. Life without Frustration. Someone should have told my father it was possible. It might have saved him a marriage and some friends.

Why should I believe what Abikẹ's half-brothers had told me? I saw her more often than they did. As for Cynthia, since the day she dropped me at home, we've barely said anything to each other. It was almost like I dreamt that night in the car. Though once, I caught her staring at me in a more knowing way than usual. A silver Mercedes slowed. I quieted my mind long enough to hand its owner an ice cream. She drove off and the thoughts returned.

Liars. All of them. Except why would their lies overlap? Watch her. Keep your eyes open. Why would they both say that she had her father's ear, his chequebook, his character? Scheming, conniving, cruel: how could they be talking about the Abikẹ that I saw every day on the road?

When I walked into the store, it took a few seconds to realise there was something familiar about the scene before me. A man was kneeling. Aunty Precious was sitting behind the counter. They turned when I entered. I saw she had been crying.

'Emeka, you have to leave.' Aunty Precious said to the man.

'But—'

'Please leave me.'

'But—'

'I'm sorry, sir, but my madam said you have to go.'

He gave her the same pleading look. She looked away. Once he was gone she began to cry.

'Aunty Precious what's wrong?'

'I can't tell you. It's not that I don't trust you. It's just—'

'Telling someone might help.'

'Emeka is the only person I've told this story. It's very long.'

'I'm not doing anything this evening.'

'What about your mum and sister?'

'They can manage for a few hours.'

143

Chapter 22

'There were some men who used to hang around outside my school waiting for girls to come out. Mr Alade was one of these men but he told me he was not looking for a girlfriend. Instead, he wanted a young seamstress to take abroad. He said the factory he was recruiting for particularly wanted Nigerian girls because they were the most hard-working. At first, I was reluctant. Although I could hand-sew well, I wanted to go to university and study medicine. I was my parents' only child and they took my education very seriously.'

'Let me get you some tissue.' I went to the small toilet in the corner and took a new roll.

'What was I saying?'

'Your parents.'

'Yes, they were village people. The world moved too fast for them, even me, their daughter. Mr Alade took one look at our small parlour and knew what would make them release me. He gave an estimate of what I would earn in a month then he converted the figure to naira. My parents were not greedy but they had always worried about paying my university fees. "Stay for two years" my father said when Mr Alade left. "Stay for two years and come back and study medicine." The day Mr Alade brought the contract we signed without reading. He said that if we read it, it would show we did not trust him. After that he made one final request. He asked that I go to a shrine to swear.'

'A shrine?'

'Yes. We too were shocked. But Mr Alade said that the man who owned the sewing company was a traditional Nigerian. So we followed him to the bush to swear. As we were about to enter the shrine, Mr Alade told my mother she could not come in.'

'Were you afraid?'

'I was very afraid. Remember I was only sixteen. When I walked in and saw fresh blood on the floor I almost ran out and said I wasn't doing again. It was the memory of the mobile phone Mr Alade promised that made me walk to the *babalawo* at the back of the shrine.'

'What did he look like?'

'I don't know. He told me to kneel down. I was too scared to look up while he listed the curses that would follow me if I broke the contract. At the end, he spat in his hand and rubbed it over my face.'

'And you let him, Aunty Precious.'

'What could I do? In any case, I was lucky. Some of the other girls later told me their *babalawo* poured his urine on them.'

'Excuse me, do you sell powdered milk?' a woman asked

from the doorway. From her olive skirt suit and square shoes, I could tell she was an employee from the new office down the road. After Aunty Precious had served her, I shut the door and put the closed sign in the window.

'Please continue.'

'By the time Mr Alade finished with us, both I and my parents were so excited. We told all our neighbours that I was going abroad. We told relatives; sometimes even strangers on the street. The only reason I was sad about leaving was Emeka. Everyone on our street used to call us husband and wife.'

'The same Emeka that just left here?'

'Yes. We grew up together. His house was just five steps from mine and I saw him more than I saw my parents. He promised to wait for me when I left. We took a bus to Italy: myself, Mr Alade and ten other seamstresses. On the way, my seat mate confessed that she did not know how to sew. I had a small sewing kit on me so I taught her. I also taught some of the other girls who were not yet perfect. I thought Mr Alade would be angry that some of us could not even do basic embroidery. All he said was it was good we were occupying ourselves on the journey.'

'How long did it take?'

'Six weeks to reach Rome. We got there in the night and for the first few months, I rarely saw the city in daylight. Some of the girls would go out in the afternoon but I was too ashamed. I felt that everyone who saw me would know how I earned money.'

It was odd that she should be ashamed of working in a

sweat shop. There were worse ways for a woman to survive in a foreign country. I wanted to reassure her of this but she had reached a point in her story where she could not bear interruption.

'The women in the house Mr Alade dropped us in said we had no choice. We had signed and sworn that we would not stop working for them, until we paid off our debt. These women that ran the house were very harsh. They enjoyed putting us down and insulting us but one was kind to me. She said I looked like her junior sister so she gave me advice that saved my life. She was the one that told me I should make sure my customers always wore a condom no matter how much they offered for sex without. A lot of the other girls took the money and died of AIDS.'

Aunty Precious hadn't gone to Italy to sew on buttons in an airless room with sixty other girls. She had gone there to become a prostitute. Like those women I saw when I left work late. They stood on the side of the road in their tight cycling shorts, sometimes bending over so their breasts could spill out of their crop tops even further. Every thought must have shown on my face because she said, 'Maybe you are too young for this story. I'm sorry I started.'

'No, Aunty Precious. Please continue.'

She was not like those girls. She had been tricked.

'It's funny. Now, when I look back on those years, what makes me the angriest is the shoes I had to wear. None of the men that beat me left scars. It's so hot in this country, I can no longer imagine what it felt like to wear a miniskirt in winter but the shoes – they have left permanent marks.

Look at my feet.'

She slid off her slippers and raised one leg. 'See how swollen they are. Look, I don't have ankles and it's because of walking around Rome in high heels. My feet used to ache so badly that I would go around the streets barefoot. Until one day, a customer beat me for leaving black footprints on his white bed sheet.'

'Aunty Precious—'

'No. Stop looking like you are about to cry. I was one of the lucky ones. I met Richard. He was old with grey hairs all over his body but he was kind. Whenever I told him I didn't feel like, he would always reply, funny enough I don't feel like either. He was a colonial officer in Kenya when he was a young man. That was why he picked me up. He said I reminded him of a Luo woman he loved. One day he offered to pay off my debt in exchange for my living with him until he died. He too drew up a contract for me to sign.'

'Did you?'

'Of course. It was about survival. But this time I read before I signed.'

I looked at her green boubou and the rubber slippers she wore on her cracked feet. When we used to travel, I'd noticed there was a type of glamorous woman you saw with white men. 'I can't imagine you with a white man, Aunty Precious.'

'Neither could his children. They were always asking if Richard had changed his will and other questions like that. We were together for two years before he passed on. One morning I woke and found he was not breathing. Coronary heart failure is what the doctor said and while his body was still warm the children swooped down to drive me away.'

'How did you survive after he died?'

'His will said, "to my precious Precious, ten per cent of all my savings". Even that little portion, his children wanted to take.'

She stopped and looked outside the store. 'You should be going. It's getting late.'

'You haven't finished.'

'What else is there? I moved to Nigeria. I set up a store with my inheritance, the same one we are in now.'

'What about Emeka? Tell me what happened when you came back.'

'You have to go soon.'

She blew her nose again.

'I looked for my parents but another family was living in our house. They had died poor, the new tenants told me. Their daughter had gone abroad and not sent them money. Shame would not allow me to go to the village and see where they were buried in the family compound. My relatives would have cursed me.'

'I'm sorry, Aunty Precious.'

'It was many years ago. I started going to church to fill time on Sundays. I joined the choir because I liked their uniform. Then one day, the preacher announced, "There is a woman sitting here. You are precious, despite what has been done to you. God has called you by that name, Precious." Many years passed, the shop thrived and I thought I had left Italy behind.

'Then Emeka walked into this store asking if I sold shaving sticks. The shock almost killed both of us. We screamed and hugged and all the time we held each other, I kept thinking, he must be married now. He must have at least two children. I pulled away from his embrace and came to sit behind the till. "So how is the wife?" I asked, preparing myself for the news. "There is no wife," he said. "I have tried to get married but no girl has been like my Precious."'

She smiled and dabbed her eyes. 'Look at me, acting like a teenager over a man I just sent away.'

'Why don't you say yes?'

'His family hates me. I left their son to go to *obodoyinbo*. I used juju to stop him from marrying and now I have come back to ruin him. To add to that, he told them that I used to be a prostitute. He thinks everyone is easily forgiving like him. Now over his sisters' dead bodies, his mother's dead body and his father's dead body, will Emeka marry me. The only way they will attend the ceremony is if we marry in a cemetery.

'It's them that almost closed down my shop. They told everyone in the area about Italy. Now the tenants upstairs would rather walk twenty minutes to another store than buy anything from me. If not for your hawking and the customers from the new office, this shop would not be open.

'When you walked in he was proposing for the fifth time. Yet, he will come back and I must say no. I will not separate him from his family and I will not ruin his reputation. He is respected in his work.'

'What does he do?'

'He is a pastor and even though the Bible mentions prostitutes who did well for themselves, no Lagos congregation would listen to that.'

'You don't have to tell them.'

'He would feel he had to. If he didn't, his family would.'

If he had worked as anything else, he could have married her and kept his job.

'Before I left Italy I visited the kind matron to say goodbye but also to find out about her employers. I took her for lunch and gave her some expensive perfume. At first she refused to say anything. She thought it was foolish to try and find such dangerous people. She grew more cooperative with alcohol. Even then, when she spoke, she would only tell me the man's name was Olumide Johnson and that she had been surprised to hear he had a daughter. When I asked where I could find him she refused to say.'

'Olumide Johnson?'

'Yes. Remember that day we went to the market, you mentioned your friend with the same surname. For a moment I thought it was his daughter, but where would you have met someone like Olumide Johnson's daughter?'

Of course.

'After I returned to Nigeria, I became obsessed with finding him but the name Olumide Johnson appeared so many times in the phonebook.'

I was glad I had said nothing.

'There was a man I was certain was him. He owned a large car business that could serve as a front. He had the political connections necessary for blinding the eyes of border police. When I went to his house and asked the gateman if I could see Oga's daughter, he said I had the wrong address. Oga only had sons.

'Eventually I found him. He was hidden behind many respectable businesses and he had even more political connections than the first Olumide Johnson. He was tall and dark with a mark blacker than the rest of his skin on the side of his face. He had a daughter. She was his only child with his wife.'

How many powerful businessmen with birthmarks could there be?

'I found a young lawyer just out of university and full of the justice he had crammed for his exams. He helped me find the others who returned to crawl into the holes in Lagos. We built a strong case that we really believed could win. Then the first of us died, then another was bought off, and another disappeared and then one day, he killed the young lawyer as well. It was made to look like an accident but we knew.'

I remembered the man in the corridor; the harshness with which he had spoken to his own son and I could believe he had killed people to cover up his crimes. Did Abikẹ suspect? Surely his favourite daughter would know what her father was capable of.

'After our lawyer died, we returned to our holes and tried to forget about the case. But at times like this, when Emeka reminds me of the woman I could have been, I want my justice.'

Chapter 23

Nkem and I were browsing through the shoe section at De Moda with an attendant trailing so close, I could feel her breath.

'Ma, you should try this one.'

'My dear, please, have some taste.' Nkem snatched the shoe and clonked it back in its place. 'Is that fashion?'

The girl shrank. 'I'm sorry, ma.'

Nkem did not hear because she had stomped ahead.

'Wait. Let me have a look at those shoes.'

The girl curtsied and handed me the right foot. Two plastic jewels adorned the front; glitter covered the heels, silver chains hung from the buckle. I waited until Nkem was beside me. 'Not bad. They have a certain sparkle. Don't you agree?'

'Well I—'

'Don't you?'

'Well, of course, looking at them properly, I see that they are quite special.'

'More than special. Unfortunately it's not the colour of my dress,' I said, placing the shoe with its partner.

When I turned, Nkem had left again, distancing herself from the scene of her disgrace.

'What about this?'

'Hmm, black shoes with a pink dress. Not very tasteful, Nkem.'

'Why do you say so?' she asked, pointing the heel at me.

'It makes me think of lingerie.'

Behind us, the attendant coughed twice.

'How about this?'

Interesting. *'Do you have anything in this colour, in a size five but with heels higher and thinner than this?'*

'Yes, ma.' She bobbed, taking the shoe and scuttling away.

'Stilettos, Abikę? Are you sure? You're going to be doing a lot of walking.'

The attendant returned with two pairs.

'Definitely the peep toe, darling.'

Some boys don't like toes. My hawker might be one of them.

'Let me try that one.'

I slipped on the closed pair.

'Maroon was a good choice,' Nkem said.

I walked around the store, testing their fit.

'Aunty, pick that one, it's very fine on you,' the attendant offered shyly.

'I'll take them.'

I have not felt this impotent since the day my father's jeep exploded. By the time the news reached us, melting iron had burned his face beyond recognition. With Aunty Precious it was not too late. I almost shouted, I know him, when she described Mr Johnson. I managed to restrain myself in time. Knowing I knew him would not change the fact that she was no closer to justice. Instead, the knowledge might trigger the process that led nowhere the first time and would lead nowhere again.

I couldn't go back to her house. Not after this. What if I ran into her father, what then? Take matters into my own hands and strangle him? I remembered the tour she gave me on my first visit; how she had lingered in the more opulent rooms and made sure I saw the indoor swimming pool. What if she knew it was all paid for with dirty money?

'You should go. It's getting late.'

'Are you sure you don't want me to stay a little longer?'

'No, I'm fine. Take some bread for your mother.'

As I sat on the bus home, I thought of Abike. For a few weeks, it seemed possible that we would end up a couple. The *danfo* swerved and jolted a woman's elbow into my ribcage.

'Sorry o,' she said. 'Don't mind this useless driver.'

'Nah who dey call me useless?'

When no one answered, the driver swerved again before letting the bus move in a straight line.

It wouldn't have worked between us. Even without everything I'd heard, the real world would have intruded. When she went to university and returned with a fancy degree would she still want a hawker for a boyfriend? When she got her first high-flying job and I was just a trader in Tejuosho would she want to be seen with me?

This is where you live, I saw as I passed the men who played snooker all day with balls cracked from overuse.

This is where you must stay, I thought, as I reached the stairwell and saw Ayo and his friends, smoking.

This is your home, I knew, as I stood in front of the scabbed door of my flat.

When I walked in, Jọkẹ was hunched at the table, a lone candle flickering over her homework.

'How far?'

'I'm fine.'

'Has Mummy eaten?'

'I don't know.'

'What do you mean you don't know?'

'I gave her beans,' she said pointing at a bowl on the table. 'I don't know if she ate it.'

I picked up the bowl and looked inside. It was full.

'Jọkẹ, how many times have I told you? When you give Mummy food, make sure she starts eating.'

She shrugged and continued writing.

'Jọkẹ.'

I took the candle and went to my mother's room, leaving her in darkness.

'Bring my candle back o.'

I knocked softly and pushed my mother's door open.

'Mummy, you haven't eaten.'

She was lying on the bed staring at the wall.

'You and your sister should stop fighting.'

'Are you going to finish your beans?'

'I've had some already. You have the rest. Good night.'

I took the candle and bowl back to Jọkẹ.

'Next time make sure she starts eating even if you have to give her the first spoon. Now she's going to bed without food.'

'What's my business?'

'You know she took his death harder than—'

'I'm working.'

She angled her chair so her back was to me.

'Don't speak to me like that.'

'Move. You're blocking my light.'

I walked into our room and flung off my shoes. I almost tore my shirt as I pulled it over my head. Finally, I sat on the mattress in my underwear, breathing heavily. I was a child again, waiting for one of the maids to put on my pyjamas for me. Waiting because I knew she would give in and pick up the pyjamas that were next to me and put them over my head. Then she would uncross my arms and push them through the sleeves. No maid would be coming tonight. I stood and started rummaging through my side of the wardrobe.

The only clothes of my father's I kept were his pyjamas. I sold everything else. My mother wanted me to save one suit but we needed the money more than I needed to look smart. The only reason I kept his pyjamas was because they had his initials stencilled on their breast pockets. For some reason, I did not like the idea of a stranger wearing his initials.

Whenever I button myself into his nightshirts, I feel his

quietness slipping over me as I slide each button into place. Tonight, it was not enough. My breath was still uneven and I was afraid that if I went out to speak to Jǫkẹ in this mood, I would lose my temper.

There were three large bags in the corner of the room. His certificates were in a Manila envelope in the third bag from the left. I drew them out and began to leaf through. First was his birth certificate, twenty-seven years before mine, then his baptism, then a silence of fifteen years before you got to his Senior School Certificate, all As, then University, second-class upper thanks to your mother. Here I stopped. This was him before me. The next certificate would turn him into my father. I knew what it was but still I took my time, maybe there would be something extra. As usual, next came Marriage, then a Masters, then Death.

These certificates should make me angry. I only have two to his seven. There is little chance of any more, except the one for death and perhaps marriage. Still, holding the milestones of his life never fails to soothe me. My father was somebody. While he was alive I may have despised him for being weak but he was still a university graduate, a Masters holder, a successful lawyer. Maybe one day Jǫkẹ will have as many or more.

I wondered if today should be the day I finally looked through the bags. I had only a vague idea of what I would find: probably our old family albums, his CDs, perhaps a few musty books. Each time I'd come close to emptying the bags, a pressing matter would excuse me from having to confront the fragments hastily packed when we left Maryland. Today was no different. I returned his certificates and went to speak to my sister.

'Jọkẹ, I don't like how you've been behaving recently.'

She dropped her pen. 'Are you going to give me a parent talk?'

'I'm being serious. On my way home yesterday, I'm very sure I saw you by the stairs with the Alabi girl talking to a guy that looked at least twenty. Also, I don't like the way you speak to me.'

The pen started moving again. 'The Alabi girl's name is Funmi and she and those boys are the only people close to my age in this whole building. Not all of us can have rich friends.'

It had never occurred to me that Jọkẹ might want to come with us. Her fourteen seemed so far from my eighteen. Now it was too late.

'You're blocking my light. Can you stand somewhere else or get out from here.'

'Don't speak to me like that.'

'Or else?'

I snatched her pen and flung it to the ground.

'Is that all?'

She unzipped her pencil case and brought out another.

'I'm not playing with you,' I said, grabbing the hand with the pen.

'Leave me.'

'I don't like the way you've been behaving. I don't like you hanging out with that Alabi girl. I don't like the way you talk to me.'

What was I doing?

I let go and the pen clattered to the floor.

'I'm sorry.'

A round spot of ink was pressed into her palm.

'You're a bully.'

She picked up her pen and continued writing.

I went back to the room, lay on the thin mattress that was our bed and closed my eyes.

When I woke the next morning Jokẹ's hand was holding mine.

Chapter 24

'Mon Dieu, *you want me to make what?*'

'A pink satin dress that starts at my neck, stops at my knees and has no back. If you can't do it I'll take my money somewhere else.'

'Ma chérie, *that design is horrible and with such material? You will look like a birthday cake, a flat-chested birthday cake!*'

The women in the waiting room tittered behind their magazines.

'Tayo, watch it.'

'My apologies. It's just that you're Abikẹ Johnson. The Mr Johnson's daughter. How can you ask le chemisier *to do this?*'

'Have it ready by next Tuesday. '

'You won't change your mind.'

The statement fell on my turned back.

'Well then, le chemisier *will have your frock ready.* Ça fait rien.'

'OK, Tayo.'

'Who's next?'

A woman who bulged in many areas approached him,

clutching a ripped page and pointing at a svelte actress.

'I want to look like this when you make her dress for me.'

'Bien sûr. C'est possible.'

It was amazing how after only spending a year in Paris, French phrases stuck to his speech.

When I got out, I saw Hassan sitting on his haunches amidst drivers that belonged to the women inside. I was proud to see his uniform was the smartest.

'Let's go.'

'Yes, ma.'

A man that was younger than the rest winked at me and asked loudly, 'Na this small girl be your madam?'

The group laughed, nudging each other and jeering at my driver.

'Yes, I be him madam. Wetin concern you?'

'Your pidgin is not bad for an ajẹ-butter.'

'Your English is OK for a driver.'

The man sprang up, his pert face suddenly stony. 'Let me tell you, I spent one year studying engineering. If not for lack of school fees I would have graduated and been driving your type of car so don't insult me.'

'And you think because of this big car I am an ajẹ-butter? I can take you round Tejuosho Market. You too don't insult me.'

I stepped forward, crossing my arms, mimicking the fighting stance of the market women I had seen in the past months. We stared at each other, waiting to see who would blink. Then one of the men called out, 'This one is not an ajẹ-butter o. She is a real child of Lagos.'

The others laughed, allowing us to join without shame.
'Madam, my sincerest apologies,' he said, dipping his head.
'Oga,' I replied with a mock curtsey, 'no vex.'
I entered the jeep and drove off into the afternoon traffic.

Once I got home, I crept up the stairs, hoping I would reach my room without running into my mother. The scent of my party has brought her crawling out of her hole. In the past few days she has been sitting in the upper rooms, slugging through the latest magazines.

'Abikẹ, I was just coming from your room.'

'Really? Good afternoon.'

She rested her hand on the banister and began to glide down, eyes trained on the hidden cameras filming her descent.

'How is the planning going? You know I can always help if it's affecting your studies at Green Lake.'

'I have a party planner and my school is called Forest House. Sorry I can't talk. I need the bathroom.' I pushed past her outstretched hand.

'But—'

'I'll come down later.'

'Be quick. I'm starting Matters of the Heart *at four.'*

When I got to my room, my phone rang. For a second I thought it would be my hawker then I remembered he didn't have a phone.

'Hello, Oritse.'

Where is he?

'That's great you've written a new song.'

He was supposed to come today. It took me three hours to

realise I had been stood up. On the way to Maison du Tay I was furious. There was a birthday lunch I'd missed waiting for him. Then I remembered the many things that could have gone wrong in the week we hadn't seen each other. He may have been hit by a car.

'Oritse, we'll talk about you playing at my party later.'

He might be ill.

'That sounds good.'

Or something may have happened to his mother.

'OK. Bye.'

I'll stop at his flat tomorrow with an invitation.

I was supposed to go to her house today.

'Runner G, wetin you want chop?'

Instead I went to the *buka* to hang with the boys. I hadn't seen them in weeks and they had grown scruffier in the time, a little menacing.

'Thanks, but I'm not hungry.'

A girl bounced past, her two-tone denim jeans straining at her thighs.

'Omo, that babe is sweet.'

'Runner G, you like that one?' asked a man who sold plastic kittens from China.

I made a noncommittal noise and looked round the buka. It was a Saturday afternoon. The place was empty, with the bare plastic tables showing oil and grease stains.

When a glittering Mercedes jeep drove by, we all stopped to watch its curves glide through the air. Once the dust settled the MTN recharge card man was the first to speak.

'One day, I go drive car like that.'

'Yes o.'

'Amen,' the others murmured. I was silent.

'Runner G, you no want car like that?'

'You don't know what he did to get that car.'

He was either in debt like my father or he was a criminal.

'How you know?'

I shrugged.

Aunty Precious knew.

She was more reserved now. Whenever I went to the shop, awkward gaps hung between the pleasantries we managed to exchange. Yesterday she caught me looking at her and mumbled, 'I shouldn't have told you.'

I did not know how to explain that what she saw in my face was not judgement. Aunty Precious was ashamed while the man who had filled brothels in Europe was a respected member of society.

'Runner G, where have you been ensconcing yourself?' said a man who hawked *Oxford English Dictionaries*.

'I've been around.'

'I hear say one rich girl dey block you. That's why you no dey come here any more,' said an apple seller.

'I don't know what you're talking about.'

'Oh boy talk true, jo,' said a man who sold calculators from Taiwan.

'She dey pay you?' the MTN man asked, gesturing and leering at the same time.

I stood.

'You know what, I should be getting home. It was nice to see you guys.'

'You know we are just playing.'

'Just adding a little ribaldry to the afternoon.'

'Abeg, Runner G, sit down.'

The MTN man reached for my arm; I took a step back and bumped into the Mama Put who owned the buka.

'You no go eat?' she asked in the special, soft voice that she used for me.

'I have to go. I'm really sorry.'

'Stay and try some of my stew.'

'No, I'm sorry.'

'Oya, wait and take this.'

As she reached into her bra I began to move back. I was not fast enough. The fried meat was already in her hand.

'No, thanks. I'm not hungry.'

'Just take this small one,' she said, coming closer.

'Look, I don't want your meat.'

I turned and walked away, the boys' shouts ringing behind me.

'Runner G, why you waste that meat like that?'

'Why you no give me?'

'Aunty, don't mind the useless boy. Give me instead.'

What was I doing with these people?

Chapter 25

We've had a fight: petty, and ridiculous, just like any argument that for no reason escalated into a common brawl. When I arrived at his house with his invitation, the jeep attracted some stares and a handful of children. There was no one like that tout, Fire for Fire, in sight. I climbed up the stairs, knocked on his door; he opened it and said, 'What are you doing here?'

'It's good to see you too.'

His chest was barely covered by the worn singlet he had thrown on. A bread crumb, perhaps from breakfast, rested on his left cheek. I was tempted to brush it off.

'How did you get here?'

'My driver drove.'

'Your driver?'

'Yes, my driver.'

'So you came here in that, in that monstrous car of yours.'

'If that's a question then, yes, I did. Are you even going to ask why I'm here?'

'Are you going to tell me why you are putting my family in danger?'

'What are you talking about?'

'What am I talking about?'

This was getting ridiculous. 'Yes. What are you talking about?'

'Do you not live in this city?'

'Do you?'

We were having an argument about whether or not I lived in Lagos. I had to be missing something.

'What's wrong?'

'What's wrong? I'll tell you what is wrong.'

'Tell me then.'

'It's you.'

An apartment door opened. No head appeared, just a voice. 'Can you be quiet? My baby is sleeping.' A wail drifted down the corridor and the door banged shut.

From then on, we conducted everything in a low hissing.

'It's you,' he said again, speaking through clenched teeth. 'Bringing your car and attracting the attention of every tout in this area. Don't you know you're marking out my block for armed robbers?'

'Don't you think you are exaggerating?'

'Exaggerating? What do you know of life in this city? What do you know of poverty or being forced to listen to your neighbours getting shit beaten out of them every night for a few hundred naira?' Flecks of saliva began to dot his lips.

'I know that you are over-reacting. I can tell my driver to

move the car.'

'Your driver. The man doesn't have a name? Why are you here?'

'I come to visit you in this hell of a neighbourhood and it's just now you're wondering why I'm here.' I squeezed his invitation into my fist.

'So that's your opinion of where I live?'

'If you love Mile 12 so much why are you always in my house?'

'You think coming to your house is the only thing I can do on a Saturday? How dare you use that to insult me?'

'Useless boy. Who are you? You think you're so wonderful because you support your family. You think they should make a movie out of you, don't you? Telling me how you ran for the first time, how much you've improved. Well trust me, you're going to need to do a lot better if you're ever going to get out of this dump.'

An ace.

'Leave this place.'

Match point.

'I'm going. I wouldn't want to endanger your mother and sister any further. It's bad enough having you for a provider.'

Game: Ms Johnson.

He slammed the door and chips of hardened wood fell to the ground. When I got outside, the children were swarming around my car. There was not an adult in sight. Bastard.

She called me useless: a word for bent spoons and broken

toys. I used to call my father useless when I saw him with his legal friends. He was supposed to make me proud to be his son. Instead he dithered at the edges of conversations, looking for whose glass was empty.

I have always thought I am the opposite of him. It has encouraged me to think he would never have survived as a hawker. Maybe despite all this, I am still useless. I try to look after my family but it is not enough. Jọkẹ's trousers ride above her ankles and my mother refuses to eat the coarse food I put on our table.

Abikẹ has certainly studied me long enough to know what will make me doubt myself. Or it may have been chance that led her to that word. I should have invited her in to hear why she came. How could I with Aunty Precious's story so fresh in my mind? No. It was good I left her outside. Just a few minutes standing in my corridor and her real thoughts came out. I am just another servant. Maybe I am even 'my hawker' like Hassan is 'my driver'.

I blame my father. If he had taken the time to service his car then a girl younger than me wouldn't be able to insult me so thoroughly. On the day of the accident, his tyre burst and he lost control of the car. It skidded down a bank and rammed into a tree. Not long after, it caught fire. The police report said this was because the car had not been serviced properly.

He never drove fast, always stopped at traffic lights and in the end he forgot to service his car. It was just like him to fall at the last hurdle. Court my mother for five years and agree to end it once my grandfather said no. Slave away in law school to become a paperwork man instead of making a name in court. Useless.

I have finally seen the Abikẹ that her half-brothers and Cynthia see. I wonder how she has kept her hidden for so long. I should be flattered by the effort.

Chapter 26

'Taste this.'

'Too much hoisin, dear.'

'You think?'

'Of course! All these restaurants destroy Chinese delicacies to please the Nigerian palette. It's disgusting.'

It was the fifth restaurant and it seemed no Chinese in Lagos would do. In Jade Pavilion, their stir fry did not have enough water chestnut; in Mr Wong, the sesame seeds looked stale; in Madam Chi they had served us duck with plum sauce not hoisin. Plum sauce!

'Nkem, I think this will do.'

'What—'

'Don't worry, my guests can't tell chow mein from spaghetti.'

'Abikẹ darling, you are so funny.'

'How much will this menu cost for a hundred and fifty guests?'

The manager drew out a calculator from his trouser pocket. His face transformed when he saw the figure.

'One million, fifty thousand naira. For you,' he paused, unable to speak and smile so widely, 'for you, we will do one million.'

One million, for greasy noodles that didn't even have water chestnuts?

'Abikẹ darling, that's a good price.'

With that you could buy ten years of hawking.

'I can't go any lower.'

'As your planner, I advise you to consider this offer.'

A hundred stalls at Tejuosho.

'Only one million naira,' he said loudly enough for heads to begin to turn.

'Take it.'

Of course Nkem was right. A million was only four thousand pounds, a handbag.

'Write the bill to Olumide Johnson and send it here.' I gave the man my father's business card.

'Yes, madam.'

As we left, a few diners abandoned their meals to look at the girl who had just spent one million naira on noodles. I saw no judgement on their faces.

'So there's the food sorted out. Now we have to start thinking of a DJ, and the outer decor. Nothing ostentatious but it would be lovely to have some petite fairy lights dangling from the trees.'

'I don't need fairy lights.'

'How come, darling?'

'I want it in the afternoon.'

'You said—'

'I've changed my mind.'

All this was so stupid.

He wasn't coming and so I didn't want one hundred and twenty-six people filling my house. There was no question of cancelling: the news had gone too far. But over my dead body would they spend more than three hours dancing.

'So do you now want the party inside or outside?'

'Aren't you the planner?'

For a second on my hawker's doorstep, the argument had seemed like just another round of Frustration. I could not stop myself. By reflex, I was playing.

'Abikẹ, since you want it in the afternoon, maybe we could hire a small live band. I know it's a bit avant-garde but there's a certain je ne . . .'

Listening to Nkem run on, I wondered when exactly her voice had begun to grate.

Today, for the first time, I fought on the road. I only meant to threaten the man but when he shoved me in the chest, my fingers closed round his collar. After that there was no going back. Only a few blows were struck before a crowd came to separate us.

'Wetin be the matter?'

I explained to the old lady that the man had cheated me.

'Nah so?'

The thief shook his head. 'No be so. His money complete.'

I could see some touts approaching. Once they reached

us, they would extort more than what I was struggling for.

'O boy, use the twenty naira buy toothbrush. Your mouth dey smell.'

As I walked away, I wondered what Abikẹ would have thought if she had seen me. Usually it is my mother's opinion I reach for whenever I have done something shameful on the road.

'Sss!'

The woman calling me was in a red Toyota Camry. Her synthetic hair matched perfectly the colour of her car.

'Sss!' she hissed again, beckoning. I waited till her lane was about to move before shouting, 'Didn't your mother teach you to say excuse me.'

Two weeks ago, when Aunty Precious's story was fresh, I went to bed with my mind filled with anger, and injustice and hatred for wrongs. Last night it was Abikẹ I thought of before I slid into sleep. I wish I had not asked why Aunty Precious was crying that night. I cannot help her. Only she can decide to ignore what people will say and marry Emeka. She has gained nothing from telling me. I have lost.

Chapter 27

We were driving down my hawker's road and I found myself searching for him. He wasn't under the bridge. He wasn't on the side of the road.

'Hassan.'

'Yes.'

'Don't take this way any more.'

'Are you sure, Aunty?'

It was strange to see such concern on my driver's face.

'Yes. I'm sure.'

I always imagined we would remain friends. With Cynthia, I suppose she will go off and start her own set. I can only hope Oritse will grow tired of pestering me. The rest will find someone else to follow. But with the hawker I was certain things would be different.

My eyes wandered to the side mirror. There was a tall boy, holding a rack or was it a sack, running towards my car. It looked like my hawker. It was my hawker.

'Hassan! Slow down.'

'You want buy something?'

'Please slow down.'

He brought the car almost to a standstill. The cars behind honked wildly but we kept our pace. He was growing bigger. He was coming. After treating me like trash. He refuses to speak to me or visit me or find a call centre then one day he deigns to chase after my car.

'Speed up.'

'Pahdoomi?'

'Now.'

We picked up speed. He was growing smaller again. Good. He was still running though. He was gone. Where did he go? I looked at the other side mirror. He was standing on the side of the road. He had given up so easily. No. He was back again. His sack was gone. He'd left it on the side of the road for me. Somebody could steal it. All his investments gone like that.

'Hassan! Slow down!'

Wait. Maybe the fight had saved us from starting something that we could not finish.

'Hassan, drive a little faster.'

What would happen when I went to university? Would I look at him one day, like I look at Aunty Grace, someone who I once loved but have outgrown?

'Hassan, why have we stopped?'

'Oya, leave this car.'

'Pardon?'

'I said leave this car.'

How dare this man?

She was playing with me. I deserved it. The ice-cream sack was gone. It'd probably be stolen. I didn't care. All I had to do was get to that car. I almost didn't recognise it because the windows had been tinted. Luckily, I remembered the numbers on the plate.

She was speeding up again. The car was almost on the highway. I kept going. Running stopped me from having to think. Once the routine was over I couldn't hide from what I knew: it was my fault. I had driven her away when she came to see me.

The car had stopped.

'Abikẹ.'

The door opened and something fell to the ground. I'd been running full speed for almost a minute. My legs pumped faster. She would have to come out if only to pick it up.

The door shut.

'Abikẹ.'

The car flooded into life.

'Abikẹ!'

It drove off.

I slowed to a jog, still waiting for her car to reappear. I reached the express before I could make myself turn back. Why toy with me before leaving? A small bundle caught my eye as I passed the place her jeep had stopped. It stood out, shinier than the rest of the asphalt. I looked right, darted into the road, grabbed the bundle and ran back to safety.

It was money. Six thousand in fresh two-hundred-naira notes. I once told her this was how much my ice-cream sack was worth. I almost flung the money into the road. Almost. There was no need to throw away my performance prize. I crumpled the fresh notes into a ball, clutching them tightly as I walked back to where I'd left my ice-cream sack.

It had probably been stolen but I had to make sure. No, it was still there. Not because Lagos had suddenly become an honest place but because Mr T was standing over it, watching.

Chapter 28

Of late, I've been asking myself why I continue playing. My father can't disown me like he has done to some of his other children. I am legitimate, my name will be in his will if only to preserve the image he has built over the years. I suppose I know why I started that first round when he ran over the dog. It was to shock him and show him that I could not be pushed around the way I saw him pushing around his staff and his wife and his other children. I've proved this. Why am I still in his study every Wednesday stating the obvious?

I think I believed Frustration was an induction into the 'real world'. Now this seems so foolish. My father's world has only business partners and enemies. No parents or children or friends. I am sick of this half-life. After the party, I'm stopping the Wednesday sessions. If he wants to see me, he can come to my living room. If not, we will go our separate ways.

Coming to this decision has freed me. I can now play these last few rounds with all the energy I was saving for the coming years. For the first time, it is me directing the conversation.

'I think we should invite your wife to our Wednesday ses-

sions,' was my opening gambit last Wednesday.

'I wonder why you have chosen now to bring up this subject.'

'This subject is your wife, my mother. Are we not a family, the three of us? Then why must I always see the two of you separately?'

'You know how things are with your mother.'

'No. I don't know how things are with my mother because we've never discussed it.'

'Why are you asking me this?'

'How are things with my mother?'

'Things didn't work out.'

'Whose failure?'

'Things just didn't work out. It wasn't anybody's failure.'

'So what do you call it when two people who are married on paper don't sleep together, never speak to each other, never even see?'

'Maybe it was a failure.'

'So you failed.'

'Yes, I failed, Abikẹ. What else do you want me to say?'

'Why did you fail?'

'Because—' he paused and looked at the fake trophies in his cabinet. 'Because your mother did not know me when we got married.'

'Whose fault?'

'It was my fault, Abikẹ. I misled her but you understand why I did it, don't you? Sometimes you want to possess someone so badly, you trick the person into believing you're something you're not. You almost trick yourself. You can understand that, can't you, Abikẹ?'

His eyes left the cabinet and settled on me. 'In the end you can't keep up the pretence. You will slip up and once the other person discovers it was a lie, it is over.'

'Why are you telling me this?'

'As a warning, Abikẹ. That is all this has ever been. A warning.'

'The only person that needed a warning was my mother.'

He flinched then. Not like other people would flinch, just a slight twitch in his face that was quickly gone with a cover-up smile. 'But then you wouldn't be here, Abikẹ.'

'No.'

While he was hugging me good night, I noticed the almost empty bottle of wine on the floor beside his table. Maybe this was why he was so yielding. I have to win a few rounds when I am certain he is sober so I know I have learnt all I can from him.

My dress has come. I haven't looked at it. It's not appropriate for an afternoon party. I will probably wear a strappy top with a miniskirt. Now he's not coming, it doesn't even matter.

When Hassan stopped today I opened the door. I hadn't changed my mind about ending things. I just wanted to thank him for showing me round Lagos and refusing my offers to pay for lunch and standing up to Fire for Fire and spitting out the eggshell from my burnt cake when he thought I wasn't looking. Then I would lie. I would say that I was travelling for an operation and going straight to university.

Once I opened the door, I knew I wouldn't reach the goodbye. So I shut it and told Hassan never to disobey me in that way again. Our new route will reduce our journey by fifteen *minutes. It is more scenic, lined with the neat houses of the upwardly mobile in this town, bright colours that hide the blandness of the actual structures.*

The maid who brought my supper did not leave after she had put down my tray.

'Yes, what do you want?'

'Excuse me. I just wanted to know if you are OK.'

'Yes, I'm fine. The dry season makes my eyes water. Pass my bag on that table.'

There were no tissues inside. Instead, a bundle of naira notes tumbled out. Idly my fingers began counting. 9,000 naira. I rarely carry less than 15,000. I counted again. The figure remained the same. I must have spent the money without realising.

'So she left you.'

'Thanks for looking after this, Mr T.'

'And she toyed with you before she left you.'

'Long time no see. We'll talk later.'

'And from the looks of it she made sure she tipped you.' He pointed at the notes still squeezed in my hands.

'We'll see tomorrow.'

'She is the one the prophet said would come. I thought you said she was different.'

'She is.'

I didn't know if it was true any more. I just said it to make him go away.

✳ ✳ ✳

When I walked into the store, Aunty Precious asked, 'Are you OK? Why are you squeezing your face?'

'I'm fine.'

'Are you sure?'

I turned my back and loaded the leftover ice cream into the freezer.

'You can tell me.'

'I just want to get home before it gets dark.'

'Oh.'

'Good night, Aunty Precious.'

I walked to the bus stop, squashed into a small space by the conductor, and jumped from the moving *danfo* when it reached Mile 12. As I turned into my road, I saw two men fighting. If you didn't know better, you would have thought they were brothers embracing. Yet I could see the legs that were spread in fighting stance and the raised sinews that glistened with sweat. I waited to see who would topple to the ground.

'My guys, why you dey fight?' a wiry boy said, tapping a combatant on the shoulder. The man that had been tapped elbowed him in the stomach.

'Why you hit me?' the boy whined, swinging his fists between their faces. A fight of two became a fight of three, then four, then five, as people joined under the pretext of peacemaking. All I had to do was take a few steps forward. Someone's fist would catch me and then I could punch and be punched until we had all released our frustrations. I could not take those steps. No matter what Abikẹ thought of me, I had not sunk that low.

When I got to my bedroom, Jọkẹ was asleep. I slid into the space beside her, flinging the crumpled notes on the floor. Had I ever hinted that things were so bad? It had crossed my mind that she might be able to help but never seriously.

'Shut up,' Jọkẹ mumbled.

I had been speaking aloud, random thoughts falling out of my mouth.

'Stop moving.'

I rolled off the mattress and stood up, the soles of my feet cooled by the cement. As neither sleep nor calm were coming, I went to the bags. The certificates were still there, their envelope untouched. Sliding them out, I held my father's life in my hands.

June 1, 1961.

It struck me that if I tore this piece of paper, I would be destroying the only evidence that a man of his name had been born.

October 18, 2004.

It was so flimsy, such a tiny thing standing between him and death.

April 2, 1986.

I tore a corner off this one. It did not unmake me; Jọkẹ was still breathing. With a twist of my wrists I could turn the both of us into bastards.

I put them away, wondering what my father would have done if Abikẹ had thrown money at him. He would probably have refused it. For someone so timid, he could be proud. Once, a man came to the house offering a bribe. I was coming down the stairs when he said loudly, 'Don't insult me with your money.' Perhaps he heard my footsteps because his voice reduced to its normal level, leaving me sitting on a marble step, straining to hear. It was easy to be principled with a large salary. I wonder what he would have done about Aunty Precious. Probably the same as me. I can't imagine him standing up to a man like Olumide Johnson.

There was nothing stopping me from going through the bags now. I was awake. Tomorrow was Saturday. Yet even now, when increasingly I was accepting this life as normal, I was still afraid of the past. It was a seductive trap for me. During my three months at the Mile 12 school, I had wallowed in it, longing for it almost to the point of madness.

I began to pull things out of the bag and place them on the floor – albums, books, CDs, until I was surrounded. Maybe I would find a photo of my mother that would make her want to return to her old self. Maybe I would find a cheque worth millions. Then I would go to Abikẹ's house and fling her six thousand at her.

At random, I chose an album and flicked it open. It was a family picture. He was taller in my memory, Jọkẹ was thinner now and the woman in the middle was my mother. I placed the album on the ground and knelt, bending to see our faces properly. In all the pictures my father's eyes shied away from the lens.

When I got to the end, I flicked open another album. It was of a trip to America. The first page had a picture of an infant Jọkẹ, the second had a photo of me. On the third, an envelope lay where a photo should have been. I bent closer, and saw my father's handwriting.

Dọtun

His best friend was called Dọtun. They knew each other from university and had remained friends. I saw his daughter Fadeke so often that at one point, I thought she was my cousin. Yet she too was amongst the people that disappeared with his death. At least she had a good reason. The whole family moved to America not long after the accident. I turned the envelope to the front. It was already open. It must have been my mother who put it in the bag. Jọkẹ would have told me if she'd found something like this.

I drew out the letter and unfolded it carefully. The writing was his. I recognised the large letters with curling tips. Shining the torch on the left corner, I read.

Dọtun

You were always the sharper one. Even now, as I write this, I don't know how I could have been so naive. On the surface everything was straightforward. A multinational wanted to bid for a government contract. My client was to act as their representative in Nigeria. Should their tender be successful, my client was to be paid 15% of the contract value. All I had to do was help draw up a written agreement for both parties to sign.

I liaised with the lawyers abroad for weeks, going over the details of each clause. The contract we finally came up with was very favourable to my client. When he signed, I thought my dealings with him were over. Three days later, he called, asking that I follow him to Abuja. He was going to place his bid and he wanted a lawyer with him. I was surprised by how quickly he had gained access to the Minister. We took his jet to Abuja. The meeting was at 7 p.m. Dotun, if you were the one, you would have guessed immediately what was coming next. I had no idea.

There was no meeting. My client had come to offer the Minister a bribe of 100 million dollars in exchange for his multinational getting the contract. They started talking about accounts and instalments. As a corporate lawyer, you soon learn that the less you know about such agreements, the clearer your conscience. I made my mind drift off and the next thing I heard was, 'My lawyer will bring you 20 million dollars in cash next week.' I looked around. There were only three of us in the room: the Minister, myself and my client. The lawyer they wanted to carry the bribe was me.

I nodded dumbly while they discussed how I would ferry the money. I said nothing all the way to Lagos. The next morning I went to see the chief partner in my firm, Tade Olukoya. I told him that what I was about to say might come as a shock to him. Even now, I did not fully believe that one of our largest clients was trying to draw me into criminal activities.

Dotun, he laughed. Then asked if I thought my salary was paid from the proceeds of divorce cases and property disputes. He told me that my client was very impressed with my work on the contract. That was why he had taken me to Abuja. Many more opportunities would come if I did as instructed. I said I was sorry. I was willing to assist my client in a legal capacity. I *would not carry the bribe.*

I thought it was over. My client would find someone else and life would go on. Dọtun, I was so foolish. I really thought they would let me go. It started with anonymous phone calls. A voice would say, you are playing with fire, Emmanuel, then the line would cut. This happened for a few days. Then I started receiving brown envelopes. Sometimes they had brief notes inside. Other times they had small toys. One had a plastic gun, another a bomb. I told my boss. He told me to do as my client asked and we could all move forward.

Dọtun, you know I am not a brave man but I cannot carry that bribe. I think of everything I have taught my son and I cannot do it. The deadline my client gave me has passed. The calls are getting more frequent. I am tired of being prodded in the chest. There are still a few law-enforcement officers in this country bold enough to take on my client and the Minister. If they will not give me peace, I will not give them peace. Secretly, I have been going through the company files and I have found enough about my client to put him in prison for many years.

As I embark on this journey, I feel someone else should know what I am about to do. I can't tell my wife yet. I don't want her to worry until it is necessary. I can't tell my colleagues. I can't tell Mr Olukọya. It's only you, Dọtun. I don't think they will kill me. I am not being naive this time. It's true. There are many people that have died for knowing less than I do now. But increasingly, I can list those that have taken on men like my client and won. Remember Charles Nnaji and how with one phone call to the right newspaper, he brought down Senator Ike. Things are changing. Anyway, Dọtun, if I don't fight

back, they will keep growing bolder. They may target my fam-
ily. I have to act now before it is too late.

My telling you is only a precaution. Just in case. You know I
was always the most cautious in our group. You have read this
far. You can still turn back and not find out my client's name.

I flipped to the next page.

I knew you would turn over. The multinational is Centreno
Oil. The Minister is Tajudeen Danladi, Minister of Petro-
leum. My client is Olumide Johnson. The name is common
but you will know him by a spider-shaped birthmark on his
temple.

Ema

Chapter 29

I walked into my mother's room and switched on the light. She was in bed but her eyes were open, staring at the door.

'Did you read this and hide it?'

'I knew you would come. I heard the bags.'

'Answer me.'

I was shouting. Not caring if Jǫkẹ woke, or the neighbours heard, or my mother was afraid of me.

'I am still your mother. Grown as you are, you were not there when I gave birth to you.'

'Why didn't you tell me about this letter?'

'Your father's firm used to have an annual Christmas party. I met Olumide there. He didn't tell me he was a client and I didn't ask. All I knew was that he was more interesting than the people I saw every year. We started talking. He took my number. I didn't tell your father. I thought nothing of it.'

'And then?'

'And then, I – then your father started keeping late nights. He would go to work and not come back till midnight, sometimes 1 a.m., 2 a.m. Where have you been? Why so late? He would brush my questions aside. I didn't have any-one to talk to and Olumide kept calling me. He had a way of drawing things out from you. I told him about how your father was always coming back late. One night when your father was sleeping, he said just once, "Report". I told Olumide about it. I made a joke. Maybe your father was going to come clean about his mistress. Something like that. I didn't know he was listening.'

'How did you get a letter addressed to Uncle Dotun?'

'He brought it to me just before he went to America. He said he was not the man your father thought he was. He could not risk his family but he could not destroy the letter. When he tried to tear it up, it felt like he was killing your father again so he brought it to me so it could kill me. Please don't go.'

'I need to thi—'

'It was my fault.'

'They would have gotten to him anyway. It wasn't any-thing you said.'

I did not want to comfort her. I wanted to shake her and ask how she could have been so foolish. But I had grown used to speaking to her as though she was a child. Instinct-ively, the soothing words fell out.

'Don't cry. It's OK.'

'I killed him. They staged the accident but I killed him.'

Chapter 30

'I would rather die than wear this.'

That could be arranged.

'Of course it looks great on you, Abikẹ.'

I nodded, wishing for once the girl would show a little resentment. We were in one of my wardrobes and Cynthia was looking for something to wear to the party.

'How about this?'

I looked up from my phone.

'Not that one.'

'Why? I think it would fit me.'

She was standing nearly naked, overworked pants struggling to keep her bottom decent. In her hand was the miniskirt I wore on my first date with the hawker.

'No.'

'You don't even wear it.'

'You are borrowing my clothes so I tell you which ones you can and cannot take. Besides, you'd never be able to squeeze yourself into it.'

Without realising, I had snatched the skirt from her and my

knuckles were closed round it. I flung it back at her.

'You can wear it. In fact, keep it.'

She bent to pick the skirt. When she stood there was a smile on her face.

'Thanks, Abikẹ.'

I suddenly felt ashamed.

'Come with me.'

I took her into the room where I kept my real wardrobe.

'Take anything you want. Just make sure you tell me.'

'Are you sure?'

Her hands were already fingering gowns that could bear no relation to a party that started at noon.

'Of course. Wait here for me. I have to call Oritse. He wants to sing something he's written for me at the party. That boy just doesn't understand no.'

In his own understated way, my father was a braver man than I will ever be. Growing up, it was always my mother I ran to whenever someone at school tried to bully me. I was surprised by how easily she crumbled after he died. I am even more surprised that she let Olumide go. She had the letter. She had everything she needed to bring him down. Why did she do nothing?

'I was afraid.'

'I wanted him to leave us alone.'

'I didn't want you to become orphans.'

This last was ironic. I have not had a parent since we moved to Mile 12. All she needed to do was make one phone call. Now there's a new minister with new scandals. Even if someone listened, who would believe a hawker? At least then she was the widow of a promising lawyer who had just been murdered. Now we are nobodies.

He tried to make provision. The will mentioned a life insurance policy. When my mother went to the insurance company, she was told my father had missed his last payment. His colleagues and friends gave her money in the months following his death. As they soon grew tired of reminding her, they had their own families to look after. She tried to get in touch with her relatives. Sixteen years had passed, her parents were long dead. Some cousins sent a few thousands, none came for the funeral.

'We were in debt. School fees were expensive and so were the holidays. You had to have them because all your classmates had them. Then there were his relatives, always coming to the house with one problem or the other. If not school fees, then somebody was getting married. If not a wedding then a funeral.'

What did my father feel in those last few minutes? Was he tied down or did they kill him before they set the car on fire? I hope it was the second. I ran my hand through the gas flame today but still I cannot imagine.

Chapter 31

The garden in Forest House was the only good thing about having a white principal. The Nigerian before him had not cared for flowers. Instead he wanted discipline and results, things that could never be as en vogue as a white man. Mr Okon, a capable principal, was replaced by Mr Roberts, an Oxford graduate who knew nothing about running a Nigerian private school. He did however know about grass. Cynthia and I often skipped lessons to come to his garden. Today, we missed Chemistry.

'Abikẹ, what if someone catches us?'

'Just be quiet and let me talk.'

I stretched out on the grass and soon Cynthia was beside me, looking up at a sky covered in leaves.

At some point I turned my head and my eyes caught sight of her profile. She was perhaps the most beautiful girl in Forest House and a question that had never occurred to me suddenly entered my mind.

'Cynthia, why don't you have a boyfriend?'

She shrugged. 'I don't know.'

'I think you and Oritse would go really well together.'

She didn't answer. I prodded her in the side. 'Don't tell me you've never thought about it. He's a handsome boy. I give my blessing.'

'You know how much he likes you. He spends so much time writing those songs for you. Sometimes—'

'Sometimes what?'

'Sometimes he even plays them for me first so I can tell him if you'll like them.'

'You're the one that's been encouraging him.'

'You could say that.'

From afar, I saw Mr Roberts approaching. We'd been caught before. Never by the principal.

'Should we run?'

I shook my head. 'Just let me talk.'

I motioned for her to lie down. For a moment I thought he would pass. His hands were dug into his trouser pockets and his head was as bowed as his slouch. He had gone past us when his eyes landed on my pair of non-regulation patent leather shoes, kicked off while I was lying down and as unnatural as a plastic gnome in that garden.

'What is this?' He traced the shoe to my foot, then to me, then Cynthia. His oily cheeks, already red from the sun, turned a darker shade.

'What are you girls doing here?'

Cynthia shrank as I sat up.

'Teacher's orders, Mr Roberts.'

'Do I look like an idiot to you girls?'

'We finished our work and so the teacher allowed us an early lunch.'

'Which teacher?'

'Mr Akingbọla.'

He peered at us. 'What are your names?'

He had only been here two months and he still had trouble placing Nigerian names to their black faces, even when the name was Johnson.

'Funkẹ Owoyẹmi and Nneka Okoye.'

'How do you spell that?'

He snapped his notebook shut and walked off.

When he had gone Cynthia buried her face in her hands and laughed. 'Abikẹ, you're horrible,' she repeated as she rolled in the grass.

I stretched again and crossed my hands behind my head. 'I told you to let me handle it.'

'Poor Funkẹ,' she said.

'Indeed.'

A silence followed and I thought she had fallen asleep when she asked, 'What about you, Abikẹ? Why don't you have a boy-friend?'

'I don't know.'

'What about your friend that comes to your house some-times?'

'We haven't seen each other in a while.'

'How come?'

'Things didn't work out.'

'Why? You guys looked really good together.'

'They just didn't.'

In the distance, the lunch bell rang.

I stood and dusted my skirt, clods of dirt showering to the ground.

'We should go.'

Ever obedient, she stretched out her hand to be pulled up.

One week has passed since I read the letter and Jọkẹ cannot understand why I've stopped leaving the house.

'Are you ill?'

'Why aren't you going to work?'

'Have you lost your job?' she asked this morning as she stood over our mattress.

'No, Jọkẹ, I haven't lost my job. Go to school, you'll be late.'

'Why aren't you coming with me?'

'Would you go if I wasn't here to take you?'

'Of course but—'

'You'll be fine. Make sure you look three times before you cross the road.'

I rolled off the bed. Friday afternoon and I was just getting up. It felt strange to be in the flat on a weekday. On Monday I had moved around restlessly, leaning against the sink, sitting in the parlour, pacing to my bed. I emptied all the bags, strewing their contents on the room's floor. I found old school reports. I found my basketball medals, Jọkẹ's old school uniform, old passports, framed photographs, loose pictures, an empty bottle of Chanel No. 5. No letter for me.

I have spent many hours trying to reconcile this new brave image of my father with the other one. I sleep with his certificates under my pillow now. They are the first thing I see in the morning and the last thing I see at night. Between his Masters and his death, a lot could have happened if not for Olumide. There might even have been a piece of paper with the words 'Senior Advocate of Nigeria'.

I went to the kitchen and took a quarter yam from under the sink, not realising my mother was behind me until she spoke.

'What are you cooking?'

'Yam pottage.'

'Can I help?'

'Yes, please.'

I handed her the knife and she hesitated. She had grown used to us refusing her.

'It's simple.' I offered the knife again, hilt first.

Her first stroke was too deep.

'No, not like that.'

She handed the knife back to me. 'I'm sorry. The maid always did the preparation.'

'Wait, let me show you.' I scraped off the bark. 'See, only the skin.'

When she was done, six disks of yam lay in the metal pot.

'Isn't that too many?' She had unwrapped five stock cubes.

'I was cooking yam pottage before you were born. Please light the stove for me.'

'You put the kerosene in the burner—'

'Where's the stove from the old house?'

'The gas was too expensive. I sold it and used the money for some things we needed at home.'

'You should have told me.'

'I did.'

After four wasted matches, the yam was boiling and we went to the living room.

'I've been thinking about the letter.'

'Let me just go and check the yam.'

'No. We need to talk. What would you say if I were to go after Olumide?'

'I don't want you to do that but . . .'

'But what?' A minute had passed and her sentence remained unfinished.

'But I would have been ashamed if the thought hadn't crossed your mind.'

'And how would you cope if I were to . . .'

'If you were to what?'

Now it was I who could not complete my sentences.

'Before you were born I used to be a teacher . . . But I have already lost my husband to this man. I don't want to lose my—'

'I only said what *if.*'

'So how do you want to do it?'

'Not in the same way as Daddy.'

'I should know. Maybe if your father had told me, he would still be alive. I would never have mentioned it to Olumide. I swear.'

'I know,' I said, standing to get her some tissue.

'I'm fine,' she said after blowing her nose. 'You don't understand how much it helps to have told somebody.'

'Yes, Mummy. Will you try and draft a CV before I come home? I'm going to start looking for a teaching job.'

'Where are you going?'

If she didn't know, she couldn't tell anyone. Not even by accident.

'Don't forget the CV. I'll be back in the evening.'

✳ ✳ ✳

I knocked at the entrance of the store and startled Aunty Precious out of sleep.

'Can I help you?' She jumped upright and smoothed her clothes. 'Oh, it's you. Where have you been? Were you ill?'

'Aunty Precious, how did the lawyer that helped you die?'

'He died in a car accident. Why?'

'My father also died in a car accident.'

'I'm sorry. You've told me before.'

'My father was a lawyer as well. He worked with an Olumide Johnson.'

'What are you trying to say?'

'The same man that tricked you into Italy killed my father.'

Aunty Precious took off her scarf and began running her fingernails down the creases.

'I hear what you are saying but you are a hawker. How could your father have worked with Mr Johnson?'

'We used to be rich. I have travelled before, I went to a private school, we had two maids working in the house.'

'How—'

'After he killed him, Mr Johnson made sure we lost everything.'

'I am sorry, but I don't see what you want me to do.'

'You said it yourself. You want your justice. I want my justice.'

'I am too old to be disappointed again.'

'Who says you will be disappointed?'

'Perhaps we could find the others.'

'How many were you?'

'Twenty at the start, three dead, six dropped out so eleven now if the rest are still alive. I have everything in my flat: sworn testimonies, signed, fingerprinted. We will get a more experienced lawyer this time. We'll send our story to the newspapers.'

'No.'

'What do you mean?'

'No one wants to listen to our stories in court.'

'There is no other way. For people like us, we can only hope that justice will work.'

'I've met him. That girl is his daughter. I've been to his house. I've seen him.'

Her struggle with this new revelation was clear. Surprise passed into excitement into a stern resignation that I had come to call her religious face.

'It doesn't matter.'

'Aunty Precious, I said—'

'It does not matter if you know him so well you have the key to his safe. I know which way is right for me. When you are ready, I will show you the written testimonies.'

Chapter 32

'How much for half an hour?'

The girl behind the counter looked up from her novel. 'We charge per hour.'

'I only need thirty minutes.'

'I'm sorry. We charge per hour.'

'A fine girl like you is not meant to be wicked. Please help me.'

'Oya, bring the money but don't tell anybody.'

I paid her and scanned the room for the best seat.

It was three o'clock in the afternoon yet the cybercafé was full with young men typing furiously. 'Dear Sir/Madam,' I read off one screen. Did people still fall for those? In the corner I saw a computer partly hidden by a jut in the wall. It would do. I typed Olumide Johnson into a search engine. After a minute's delay, fifteen thousand results sprang up.

I clicked the first.

'Born in Lagos in 1967 to Mr and Mrs Ayọmide Johnson, Olumide was an only child. In his teens the family moved to America. There he attended NYU where he discovered his passion for photography.'

The next one was wrong and the one after that.

Olumide Johnson Nigerian businessman.

A thousand results.

The first was a list compiled by a national newspaper: 'Nigeria's Top 20 Powerful Men'. Olumide Kayode Johnson placed fifteenth.

It had no photos, no names of the companies he owned.

Olumide Kayode Johnson Nigerian businessman.

A hundred and fifty results.

This time there was a picture of him.

I read the text.

'Yesterday, in an unexpected development, Olumide K. Johnson outbid all the competitors for the chief stake in National Petroleum. He will join the Board of Directors as the controlling shareholder.'

I skimmed the rest, clicked back and continued down the page.

Most of them were about business deals and stock prices. His front was not a façade.

I opened a page that listed all the companies he either owned or was a major shareholder in.

Olu Foods.
Bataki Paper.
Lamido Farms.
Johnson Mills.
Alpha Records.
Oilet Grand Insurance.

It could not be. I refreshed the page. There it was again, number six out of thirty. It did not mean Mr T had worked there. Yet the possibility of all three of us being connected was appealing. The pattern would look like a divine sanction to Aunty Precious. I cleared my history and logged off. It would not take me long to find out if he was lying.

Chapter 33

The intercom rang.

'Cynthia, please get that.'

It was the maid calling to ask where we wanted to eat. 'You guys go and eat,' I said to Cynthia, Oritse, Chike and Toyin. 'I'll join you in the dining room in a few minutes.' They left and I continued reviewing my growing guest list. To the best of my knowledge, Ikemba Okoye was coming but there had been no RSVP.

'Hello, Abikẹ.'

My hawker was standing at the entrance to my living room, wearing our pink shirt.

'Long time no see.' I stood, breathing slowly until the pounding in my chest slowed.

'Abikẹ, I'm sorry,' he mumbled at the floor. 'I've been very confused in the past few weeks.'

'Sorry for what?'

'For the way I treated you.'

'And?'

'And not coming to see you. Abikẹ, I'm sorry.'

There's no doubt what Abikẹ would have said next. I didn't want to be Abikẹ any more, at least not with my hawker. I walked to him and took his head in my hands. He shuddered but he didn't pull away.

'Don't call me Abikẹ again,' I whispered. 'Abby from now on.'

A name just for him, so that whenever he called me, I would remember that we didn't play the game.

I couldn't see his expression. I didn't want to. We stood there, my lips brushing his ear; his breath growing heavier, his lips gently pressing into my collar bone. Suddenly, his arms snaked out and pulled me to him. I raised my head. I thought he was going to kiss me. Instead, he released me abruptly and sat on the sofa.

'Abby, tell me how you've been.' He was composed now, so composed he didn't even stumble over my new name. I tried to hold his gaze. It was a draw. Our eyes left each other at the same time and I sat down beside him.

'I'm having a party in two weeks and it would be nice if you came because—'

I rested my head on his chest. When the others came back from their lunch, I didn't move.

We decided I had to go back to her house.

First I went to Abẹ Bridge but Mr T was not there. I waited on his cardboard watching the passers-by who looked at the sign SIT HERE AND CARRY MY CURSE, then at me, then once more at the sign before shifting their gazes. Finally, I saw him.

'Mr T.'

'What are you doing here? Can't you read?'

'I want to ask you something.'

'I don't want to carry your curse,' he cackled, pointing at the words he had scrawled.

'What was the name of the insurance company you worked for?'

'Keystone Insurance,' he said, sliding down next to me, his smile gone. 'Why are you asking?'

'Keystone Insurance?'

'Yes, Keystone. Do you know it?'

'I thought you said Oilet Grand.'

'That's it! Oilet Grand. I worked there for eight years and they fired me just like that!'

I stood up. What had I been thinking coming here? Rush-hour traffic was building which meant it was already past five o'clock. I still had to get back to Aunty Precious. 'You're wasting my time, Mr T.'

'Wait!' he said, grabbing the hem of my trousers. 'I'm not lying.'

'So why don't you remember your employer's name?'

'I know I worked in an insurance company. I worked in claims. Work started at eight. There was a revolving door at the entrance. We ate lunch from 12 to 12.30. The man who sat opposite me, his name was Bode. But I can't remember the name of the company. In my head there's a signboard. Sometimes it flashes Oilet, sometimes Keystone, sometimes

Liberty, sometimes all three.'

'How do I know your mind didn't just flash this story five minutes ago?'

'Ask me something? Anything else and I'll tell you.'

'Who was your CEO?'

'It was a white man. No! Not a white man, an African with a white man's name. Peters or Smith or something.' He drew his knees to himself. 'I can't remember.'

'Was it Willoughby?'

'Yes!' he screamed, jerking himself upright.

I shook my trousers free from his grip. 'You're a liar. His name is Johnson. Olumide Kayode Johnson.'

'What is your business with my CEO's name? Olumide Kayode Johnson,' he muttered. 'Johnson. I know that name. Johnson. Johnson. Johnson.' He rubbed his head.

'Johnson.' He looked straight in my eyes. 'That's your girl-friend's surname. Somebody has to pay with a daughter. Tell me about her.'

'She has nothing to do with this. Go away, Mr T. My friend and I will handle this.' I patted him where his shoulder poked through his clothes. 'We're doing it for you as well.'

'Doing what? What are you going to do to Mr Johnson?'

I turned and began to walk towards *Aunty Precious* BLESSED FOOD STORES. When I looked back, he was shuffling to his cardboard.

✳ ✳ ✳

'I've taken what you said about using lawyers on board,

Aunty Precious, but after looking into the matter further, I just don't think we can touch Mr Johnson that way. That's the mistake my father made. He has too many resources. We have to go through the back door.'

'How old are you?'

'Pardon?'

'I said, how old are you?'

'Eighteen. If we start—'

'The first time I met you, the day you came and made your presentation, you said you were twenty.'

'Aunty Precious, if we can get in touch with the right people—'

'I know why you lied about your age. You wanted to be taken seriously, but this matter is too serious for a teenager. I was wrong to ask for your help.'

'Aunty Precious, listen to me. If—'

'No, you listen to me. What Mr Johnson may or may not have done to your father—'

'Not may.'

'It is possible that the explosion was really an accident.'

'The letter—'

'The letter was not for you. What he may or may not have done to your father is in the past. My years in Italy, they are also in the past. Now we have to move on.'

'Aunty Precious—'

'Your father would not want you to do this with your life. You must forget this.'

'No. He cannot forget.'

Aunty Precious started at the man who had joined us.

I too was surprised but more annoyed with myself for not realising I was being followed. I saw him through her eyes: ragged, likely to grab something from her shelves at any moment. To me, he looked calmer than I had ever seen him: his speech measured, his tone soft and matter of fact.

'Who are you?'

'Don't worry, Aunty Precious. I'll ask him to—'

'Good afternoon Madam. My name is Thomas Ọlawọle. Even though my present apparel belies it, there was once a time you would have been glad to welcome me into your shop. It is for this reason I have come to tell you that you cannot talk this boy out of what we must do.'

'You know this man?'

'Not only does he know me, we have sworn to see justice done to Mr Johnson.'

I looked at Aunty Precious; she looked at Mr T. He must have stood outside, eavesdropping until he heard a fitting cue.

'What did Olumide Johnson do to you?'

Mr T raised his stump and she gasped. It was then I decided to let him speak. If she would not be convinced by what had happened to us, then maybe Mr T's lies would persuade her.

'It is not just for his own personal reasons that my friend is pursuing Mr Johnson. You see—'

He stepped forward and began to speak. I recognised the outline of the story but many of the details were new to me. His daughter became autistic, his wife an adulteress, he was personally targeted after a refusal to alter paperwork. When they cut off his arm the anaesthetic wore off. When he buried his daughter her face had already rotted. He glossed over the prophet, the most dubious part of his story. They met on the road not in the bush. Instead of a prophecy Mr T had a dream that was interpreted for him. I could see the holes, the inconsistencies, the pauses where his imagination leapt into new territories. Yet, as he spoke, Aunty Precious's face softened and collapsed into tears.

'Is this true?' she asked after Mr T had given his last flourish.

I could not do this without Aunty Precious. Without her support, her money, I was finished. Even if Mr T was mad, my story was real, hers was true, they were justification enough.

'Yes, it's true,' I said, looking into her eyes.

'You knew and you didn't tell me?'

'I didn't know it would make a difference.'

'This man has done too much evil to get away with it.'

'Yes, Aunty Precious. He mustn't get away.'

Chapter 34

It occurred to me while we were going over our checklist that I knew nothing about this woman who knew that I was allergic to prawns, that I preferred sweet to savoury peanuts; that I hated rap.

'Nkem, tell me about yourself.'

'What do you mean?'

'What's your story?'

'Well, I'm the last of four children. Both my father and mother were civil servants but they are late, God rest them. I attended the University of Nsukka, studied mass communications; and I moved to Lagos three years ago. I tried my hand at journalism but the pay was too petit for my taste. I've always adored planning parties, one thing led to another and I found myself working for Mrs Da Silva's agency.'

I had expected her to lie, a fake story that would explain her fake accent. Brought up in England, schooled there, her father was English. Instead the truth, Nsukka, civil servants.

What else could I discover before she clammed up?

'So, do you have a boyfriend?'

'No.'

'Why?'

'I can never stay with just one. They are all liars.'

'I used to think that.'

'I hope the boy that changed your mind is worth it, darling.'

'I think so.'

I smiled, remembering my new name I had made for him alone.

'Oh, you don't have to think. There are ways you can find out for sure. A few months back, a girlfriend of mine whose boyfriend had just moved back from the States, she was suspicious that the guy was cheating on her so I offered to help out. It was so easy. I called him, put the phone on speaker and with a little prompting from me, he was asking me to come and spend the night at his house. I can do the same for you. I mean because I don't know your boyfriend, one of your friends has to call him but that can be arranged.'

I am not surprised Nkem knows Frustration. She is still a novice though. By now, she should have learnt to match her story to her accent.

'Thanks for the offer but I think you should stick to planning my parties.'

Aunty Precious is not convinced. After my visit to Olumide's house she lost her nerve and brought the testimonies to our next meeting.

'What is this?'

She placed the stack of papers in my arms.

'We have to consider all options.'

She turned to Mr T. 'Don't you agree?'

'Of course, madam. Are there any more biscuits?'

'See,' she said as Mr T slotted a whole digestive into his mouth, 'someone else sees common sense.'

Mr T began to read the first testimony with Aunty Precious standing over his shoulder, brushing off any stray crumbs that landed on the pages. Did she really think this type of ink and paper were enough to convince a Lagos judge?

'I'm going.'

'Where to?'

I didn't reply.

✳ ✳ ✳

'Mr Man, how body?'

I shook hands with one gateman and then the other.

'Who you come see?'

'Abikẹ.'

One handed me the logbook. Before I could take it, the other had snatched it away. 'Abeg no disturb Mr Man. This logbook nah for people who come with car. Mr Man, get car?'

'You be correct person,' the other gateman said as the entrance slid open. 'If you get sense, you no go talk to that girl any more. She no good.'

When I walked into their room, all that was left of the brothers were gullies sunken into the vacant sofas. The TV was silent and, above me, the fan blades creaked.

'Hello,' I said, looking at the ceiling and wondering why the painter had only done half.

'Yes,' a voice said, making me step back. 'Who is that?'

From behind a sofa a head rose and turned. It was Wale.

'Ah, it's Abikẹ's toy boy returning to pay a visit.'

'Daddy's boy, I'm happy to see you too.'

'Why are you here?'

Refusing to meet my gaze, he stared at the area just below my left eye as if it would give him the answer to his question. Finally our eyes brushed.

'It's good to see you.'

He came to sit at a table and moved a wooden chair in my direction.

'Where is everyone?'

'My father has banned us from using this room.'

'Why?'

'We were getting too comfortable in his house. Why did you come again?'

'I need a gun.'

'What?'

So it was possible to shock this boy.

'I need a gun.'

'I'm guessing you are not going to tell me what for.'

I withdrew a pen and a piece of paper from my pocket. 'Please write down the address.'

114 Majid Street, Makoko.

Ask for Seun.

Tell him Chief sent you.

He slid the sheet of paper to me.

'I suppose you won't tell me how a boy like yourself knows where they sell guns.'

'I may never see you again.' It was said without malice or regret.

'I hope you will.'

'Good luck.'

I left the room calculating the quickest route to Makoko.

✳ ✳ ✳

The area was dirty. Men's trousers were stiff with mud and the edges of the residents' feet were black.

'How do I get to Majid Street?'

No one knew. Not the women who sold fish or the men who gathered in front of a crackly television watching an old match. Eventually, it was a small child that showed me. He toddled ahead, unsteady on the stray bits of tar, happy when he was sliding on the mud that paved his streets. When we reached Majid, he refused the ten naira I offered and ran back to find his friends.

'I'm looking for Seun,' I said to the man who was squatting in the front yard of 114 and smoking.

'Seun who?'

'Just Seun.'

He licked his fingers and pinched the tip of his cigarette before slipping the charred stick into his pocket.

'Who send you?'

'Chief.'

He stood, taller than I expected. 'Nah me be Seun.'

He took me down an alley running beside the house and into a small shed in the back yard. Not even a shed because it had no roof.

'Which kind you want?'

'One that can fit into a trouser pocket.'

He withdrew a pistol from a black plastic bag. 'Like this.'

It was heavy and rust was beginning to eat the muzzle. I slid it into my pocket.

'How many bullets are inside?'

He opened the magazine. 'Five.'

'How will I shoot it?'

He showed me a few times before I got it.

'No forget. Make sure you off the safety before you shoot.'

'How much?'

'Rent or buy?'

'You fit rent gun?'

His face cracked into a smile. I saw he was not much older than me.

'Yes o. You fit rent anything for this Lagos. Even air.'

'I want to rent it then.'

'One week for ten thousand.'

'Seven thousand five.'

'Eight.'

I nodded and he gave me a black plastic bag. 'Free of charge.'

As we walked back to the front of his house, I heard sirens in the distance.

'Have police come here before?'

'Only when I no fit give them their rent.'

'How you know I no go steal you gun?'

'Nah Chief send you, nah Chief go pay.'

When we got to the house front he clasped my shoulder. 'Make you use am well. No use am kill good person.'

There was a real worry in his eyes.

'Yes.'

He squatted in the same position, relit his cigarette and continued waiting for his next customer.

✳ ✳ ✳

When I reached the store, Aunty Precious and Mr T were exactly where I had left them. The counter was littered with biscuit wrappers, empty bottles and, in front of Mr T, a half-eaten loaf of bread.

'You're back.' Aunty Precious said, waving her fingers at me. 'Mr T and I have been talking. I've shown him the testimonies and he thinks—'

'We don't need those any more.'

'You must listen to the good lady. She is talking sense, you know.'

✳ ✳ ✳

When I dropped the pistol on the counter Aunty Precious recoiled. Mr T took a step closer. His hand reached to touch. I snatched it away and returned it to my pocket.

'Where did you get the money to buy such a thing? Did you steal it?'

'It's not bought, Aunty Precious. It's rented and no, I did not steal the money. A friend gave it to me.'

'You have to take it back.'

'We have to start planning,' Mr T said, shoving the papers into her hands.

Chapter 35

'Do your parents come to your parties?' my hawker asked at some point in the afternoon.

'Yes. My mother usually stays to the end but my father will only drop in for a few minutes before going back to his study. Why?'

He shrugged.

'I know it's a bit embarrassing that my parents are coming. Maybe I should uninvite them.'

'No,' he said sharply.

'OK then, they can come.'

I stood up and began to walk round the room.

'We have a hundred confirmed guests, the DJ is hired, what else have I missed?'

'Why is it in the afternoon?'

'Pardon?'

'I'm just wondering why you're having a party in the afternoon.'

'What's wrong with that?'

'Nothing, I suppose.'

'There's obviously something.' I nudged his shoulder. 'Tell me.'

'It's just that . . .'

'Yes?'

'The last afternoon party I went to was when I was twelve.'

'You think my party is juvenile?'

'No,' he said too quickly. 'I quite like the idea of an afternoon party. It's more,' he stumbled, 'relaxed.'

'Stop lying.'

'And anyway, it's too late now.'

I sat down beside him.

'So, theoretically, if the party were two months away, what else would you change?'

He shook his head.

'Play the game,' I said, nudging his thigh with my knee.

'Well—'

This shyness reminded me of the early days.

'Well, I might have it in your garden.'

That was my original idea!

'It's not too late. We'll put up some fairy lights and move the food and DJ outside.'

He was shaking his head.

'What?'

'It wouldn't be outside.'

'You said—'

'In the garden but under a canopy or something.'

'Why?'

'Insects.'

Of course. Everything would be the same just we'd push the

party forward a few hours and get a big tent. Simple.

'What are you doing?'

'Calling my planner.'

'Don't do that,' he said, reaching for my phone.

I swatted his hand and got up.

'Hello, Nkem. It's Abikẹ.'

My hawker stretched on the sofa, watching me as I spoke. 'I'm calling about the party . . . yes, everything's all right . . . There are some changes I want made . . . Can you rent a marquee and find some fairy lights? . . . In the garden . . . In the evening.'

She broke into a torrent of Igbo.

'Onye ara.'

'Nkem?'

'Anuofia.'

For once she sounded natural.

'Nkem? . . . No need to apologise . . . Yes, it is short notice . . . I knew I could count on you. Bye.'

We were sitting in the store and there were three bottles of Fanta in front of us.

'So what are we going to do?'

Of the three of us, Aunty Precious was the most likely to fall by the wayside.

'Are you thinking of backing out?'

'I just want to know what we're going to do now you and Mr T have planned the party.'

We had decided that Abikẹ's party would be the cover for what I needed to do. The noise and crowd would serve as a distraction. His body might not be discovered till the next day. At which point, Seun would have his gun back and we would be going on with our lives.

'I still think we should go after the daughter,' Mr T said.

'But you had a daughter.'

'Exactly! An eye for an eye.'

'What kind of evil man is this? To do that to an innocent girl; your friend.'

'No one is going after Mr Johnson's daughter. Aunty Precious, please calm down. Mr T, your loss was not the only one. We are going after Mr Johnson and that is final.'

I took a gulp of Fanta and almost spat it back. The heat had warmed it to a tepid saccharine.

'The prophet said I would have helpers but you must not slow me down. We must finish the plan today.'

I tried to quell the now familiar wave of irritation that broke out whenever I was with these two. Aunty Precious and her indecision. Mr T with his prophecies and his hunger that sucked in anything edible. Sometimes he was lucid, spotting holes in our plan. Other times he was silent, his eyes roaming the store for food.

'We have finished.'

I pushed the bottle towards him and left the store.

Chapter 36

While my hawker and I were inspecting the marquee, we saw the Igbo tent men and Yoruba gardeners discussing how to string up the fairy lights without damaging any plants. None of them spoke English as a first language. It was painful to watch.

'Do you want to go? I'm tired of listening to them argue.'

'Abikẹ.' It sounded like Nkem calling. Whatever it was, I was sure she could handle it.

'Let's go,' I said, pulling him away.

We've only walked in the straight garden. I've never taken him through the other side, which I've always viewed as especially mine. There is still order – the leaves are swept up and the bushes are occasionally pruned – but there is no pattern. I made sure we stumbled on the statues my father commissioned last year. He would have been pleased to see my hawker's reaction.

I left the fountain for last. We sat and watched the woman pour water endlessly into a pool that never rose past her ankles. At some point, my hawker took my hand and kissed it gently.

We stayed there for thirty minutes, an hour, two hours, I don't know. However long, it was not enough.

I went to Abby's house. It's Abby now, no longer Abikẹ. She insists and will not answer when I forget and call her by the 'old name'. Abikẹ is still there but more and more, this Abby character creeps up. Now she has named her, I watch out for her and am wary of her comings and goings. Perhaps this Abby is the one destined to become her father one day. By then, Abikẹ will be long gone from my life. It makes the thought easier when I remember there are two.

Abikẹ is blameless. She wonders why men from different tribes would fight. Yet I sense Abby was pleased with the display she caused over her fairy lights. As the bickering escalated, she took my hand and whispered something about leaving.

'Abikẹ, please can you—'

'Let's go,' Abby said, pulling me away.

The party was in a few days. My new suit hung in the wardrobe. I had tested the gun once. I went into the bush on the fringes of Lagos and fired point-blank at a tree. Something living would have been better but no wild animal would have let me come as close as I will be when I shoot Olumide. The bullet dug deep into the bark and showered a few chips to the ground.

It had been more difficult to find where he would go after he left the party. Abikẹ had mentioned a study. Yet it may not be the same room I saw Olumide coming out of when Wale took me to meet Chief.

'Make sure he is not at home,' Mr T had said. 'Then tell one of his staff that you have a message for him but you don't know how to find the study.'

When I got to the gate, I greeted both gatemen. 'Is Oga around?'

'No.'

I was about to enter when the second gateman stopped me. 'Mr Man why you want know? No be Abikẹ you come see?'

'She said we would see her father today if he was around.'

I had become expert at creating quick lies.

'You dey meet her papa already? You want marry Abikẹ? I don tell you she no good. That kind of girl will be a very difficult wife.'

Another warning to add to my list.

Next, I went to the basement.

'Aunty Grace, it's Abikẹ's friend.'

She came out beaming. 'How are you? You didn't come with Abikẹ,' she said, looking down the corridor hopefully.

'No. I got lost. I'm actually looking for Mr Johnson's study. I have a meeting with him at twelve.'

'How come Abikẹ didn't show you the place?'

'She's not around.'

'OK. Let me show you.'

On the ground floor, instead of climbing the stairs, we

went outside and walked down a gravel path. The two-storey building at the end classed as a study in this part of the world. We entered into a reception that was lined with pictures of Olumide's offices: Lagos, London, Johannesburg, New York, Amsterdam, even Beijing. As we climbed the stairs, photographs of Olumide and powerful people stared at us. Under each was a small placard: Olumide Johnson and US Ambassador, Olumide Johnson with Lagos State Governor, Olumide Johnson with President of the Federal Republic of Nigeria. I began to hope that the gatemen had been right and Olumide was not home. When Aunty Grace knocked on a door that looked like the entrance to a safe, I stepped back, ready to run. There was no outside handle, only a lock for a giant key. This must be his actual study. She knocked again.

'It's like Oga is not around o.'

'But he told me twelve,' I said, exhaling and relaxing into my role. I knocked on the door. 'Mr Johnson.' I knocked harder banging my knuckles against the unyielding metal.

'Don't be upset,' Aunty Grace said. 'You know Oga is very busy. Sometimes he has many appointments on the same day.'

I would need a ruse to make Olumide open this door wide without suspicion. It certainly could not be bashed down.

'Doesn't he have another office in the house?'

'Oh yes, he may be in his parlour.'

As we walked back to the house, we spoke a little. 'Tell your friend to come and visit me. Tell Abikẹ that Aunty

230

Grace is really missing her.'

It was cruel of Abby to neglect this woman.

'I will tell her. Don't worry.'

She took me to the same corridor I had met Olumide and knocked on the door he had emerged from. There was no reply. I knocked. Again, there was no outside handle and the door was too strong to be forced.

'You can come back later,' she said. 'I'll tell Oga that you came. Remind me of your name.'

'No. Don't disturb him. I'll be back later.'

I went to sit in the garden for fifteen minutes then I went upstairs to see Abby. I was still wondering what I could say to make Olumide open his door when the first of his garden sculptures startled me.

A bronze lion poised to spring on an antelope, two wolves fighting and last, a big cat crouched on a branch, watching a lifelike sculpture of a small wooden child. When I saw this one, I lost my footing and fell against a tree. Behind me, I heard Abby smirk. I turned my face, not wanting her to see how shaken the joke had left me.

We continued and passed into an open space. The trees stood back and no flowers blotted the grass. Halfway through this clearing was a fountain. In its centre stood a woman, her marble arms cradling a jug from which water trickled, a diamond streak flashing into the pool around her feet. My head emptied under the sound of water hitting water.

Why waste your life?

The thought came unbidden. The fountain had released a longing to see more places like it.

I saw Abikẹ from the corner of my eye. Her head was tilted upwards catching the last rays of the sun, her hands massaged her scalp and there was an assurance to her that I once had. I studied one of those hands under the fading light, tracing the veins that ran under her skin, my face so close that by accident, my lips touched her flesh.

If not for Olumide, I would have a chequebook to shield me from life in this city. I never knew the man who signed those cheques. I dropped her hand and waited for the sun to finish setting.

Chapter 37

There was a knock on my door.

'Yes, come in.'

'Abikẹ, long time.'

It was Aunty Grace, standing in my doorway like a stranger.

'Please come in.'

She had not been to my quarters since I was a child.

'Please sit down.'

She sat on the edge of the sofa.

'I wanted to tell you that I am going to my village tomorrow.'

'When are you coming back?'

'I am not coming back, Abikẹ.'

'Why not?'

'I am ready to retire.'

She had been downstairs for as long as I could remember. It had been comforting to know she was there.

'Please get my bag. It's on that table.'

She struggled to stand. On her first attempt she fell back on the sofa. 'Look at me. I'm an old woman.'

As she tried again, I reached for her arm. 'I'll get it. Don't worry.'

There was only twenty thousand in my purse.

'I'm sorry it's so small.'

'No, Abikẹ, I can't collect that from you. It's too much.'

'Please take it.'

I pushed the notes into her tough palms. It was such details that mattered when I turned thirteen. I no longer cared that she had once slept in my room so she would be there when I woke from the recurring nightmare of watching a dog run over by a black car.

'Why are you crying?'

I'm going to be alone in this house.

'Don't worry. You won't be alone.'

She had always known what I was thinking. That was why I hadn't wanted to visit her. She would instantly sense my contempt for her small life and she would be upset.

'You have your friend that you came with that day. You must be close for you to bake cake for him. You've never liked entering kitchen.'

I'm sorry I didn't come.

'I know you wanted to come. So don't cry. See I brought boiled groundnut for us.'

When I was younger, my diet, with a few exceptions, was strictly European. My mother did not want to raise a bush child so I ate potatoes and gravy and roast lamb. Aunty Grace used to say it was wrong for me not to eat Nigerian food. She would sneak me eba and pepper soup and puff–puff, *but my favourite was always the groundnuts boiled in salt water until they were soft.*

'Thank you.'

She stayed in my room for another hour. We cracked the shells and ate the purple nuts inside.

I went to Ogun State today to finalise the rent agreement with our new landlord. We cannot come back to Mile 12 after the party. Abikẹ knows where I live and even if she didn't, it would be too dangerous to be around in the aftermath. I wonder if she will miss me. My vanity wants her to. I will certainly think of her in Abẹokuta but it would be better if she forgot me. She has the resources to find us, should she wish.

When I got to my apartment block, Ade and his friends were standing by the stairs instead of sitting on their usual bench.

'Flat levy,' he said, blowing smoke into my face.

'Ade, good evening. I have already paid my rent.'

'Bros, you know we are the ones protecting this whole building. If not for us, armed robbers go already steal everything from this place.'

He seemed convinced that it was his drugged presence that kept our block safe.

'Ade, please let me pass. I don't have any money to give you.'

'You must give us,' one of his subordinates said. 'No matter how little, you must give us something before you pass.'

'Or you can bring your sister as payment.'

I don't know which one said it. Ade was their leader. I grabbed his collar.

'You want wound me?'

235

He hung limp in my grip. For all his bravado, I could feel how weak he was. The three sidekicks stood silent, shocked by this turn of events. Finally one crept backwards and picked a bottle from the ground, clutching it by its neck.

'Drop our leader.'

I checked there was no one close enough to see us properly. I brought the gun out.

'Bros no vex,' the youngest said, dropping to his knees. The other two did the same, raising their hands in supplication. Ade remained standing, refusing to kneel in front of his followers. I pointed the gun at his head.

'Join your friends.'

When he knelt down, I put the gun back in my pocket and picked up their bench. The wood was flimsy. I slammed it against the ground. It broke easily in two.

'Don't let me see any of you in front of this building again.'

Three fled. Ade remained kneeling.

'Why are you still here?'

'I live here.'

Of course.

'Get up,' I said, slapping him gently on the side of his head. 'If you know what's good for you, leave those boys and go back to school. Or else, one day, somebody will shoot you.'

I patted my pocket and went upstairs.

Chapter 38

One day left and everything is ready. The marquee is up, the fairy lights have been strung without genocide and Nkem tells me that some of her workers exchanged numbers with my gardeners. Miracles still happen. I added fifty thousand naira to her fee.

'This is for you. Don't tell Mrs Da Silva about it.'

'No really, Abikę, it's not necessary,' she said, clutching the envelope.

'You deserve it. You've done a good job.'

She hugged me, her shoulder pressing into my cheek.

'I know, with your social calendar, we'll have many opportunities to see each other.'

Maybe, I thought as I hugged her back.

Speaking of money, I have spent too much on this party. My father signed the cheque without flinching, barely glancing at the zeros that had to be written as vertical dashes to fit into the space. His pen came down and the matter was closed. Yet, this signing of a lifetime wage just so some people could dance made me uncomfortable.

Next time, I'll use a living room and ask the kitchen to do the cooking. And next time my mother will be left in the Den. She's been in my room for the past hour. Asking what I'm wearing. Then why? Then wanting to see my shoes. Then my accessories. Sitting down, waiting for me to ask about her outfit and shoes and make-up. I am tired of that woman.

Since I started working with Aunty Precious, I have saved eighty thousand naira. This afternoon, I gave the full amount to my mother in cash.

'Why are you giving me this?'

'I want you to start managing our money.'

'No. You've been doing it all this time. Whatever you are planning, I want you to stop.'

'I'm not planning anything. I find it stressful working and managing the family budget.'

'If you don't stop it, I'm going to kill myself.'

'Don't you ever say such a thing again. What if Jọkẹ should hear you? Is it not enough that she cooks for you and cleans for you and does your laundry? Must you traumatise her as well?'

'I'm sorry. I don't want to lose my son.'

'Then you better stop talking rubbish.'

That was the closest I have ever come to hitting my mother.

The money is to tide them over till she starts her job as an assistant nursery teacher. The work is demeaning for a graduate. The pay will be useful. If she puts away a little every month, they will be able to afford the rent when it is

due in two years. Of course, these plans are for if I don't return and I am hopeful about my chances of success. On his
side are money and power. On mine are a steel gun and an
element of surprise. I shut the door and went to pick up Mr
T. He was the most alert I'd seen him in a while. We came
from the BLESSED FOOD STORES side. When we entered
the shop, we saw Aunty Precious kneeling with the ox man,
crying.

I cleared my throat.

They looked up but neither had the shame to spring
apart. 'Aunty Precious, we have a lot to discuss.'

'Emeka, please can you leave us for a few minutes.'

She stood, two patches of dust chalked into her clothes.

Emeka remained kneeling and he too ignored our presence.

'Since we are now engaged, Precious, whatever he has to
say I can hear. Same with whatever anyone has to say to me
you can hear.'

His fiancée!

'Aunty Precious, we really need to talk.'

'Emeka, please just wait outside for me. Please.'

It was the third time I would watch him leaving the shop.
The difference was clear. His shoulders were square and his
arms swayed powerfully at his side.

'I just came to remind you that tomorrow at five, we're meeting here for the last time. Is there any part of the plan you
want to discuss before then?'

'As you grow older, you will learn that regret follows
everything, even the best decisions.'

'What do you mean, Aunty Precious? You are just going to forget.'

'I have not forgotten. I have just chosen to live my life in a way that honours the people I loved. Do you think your father would want to see you like this? With a cheap gun you rented from a good-for-nothing criminal.'

'You know nothing about my father.'

'And you don't know anything about Michael or what I went through in Italy, years ago, when you were still a child. So don't think you know something about me because I have been your boss for a little over a year.'

'Madam, please, a bottle of Fanta for a poor beggar.'

All this while, Mr T had been listening. That he had chosen to speak, I took as a sign to change tactic.

'How will Emeka's friends react when they find out?'

'His true friends already know.'

'What of his congregation? What will they say?'

'I never thought you would use the things I told you that night against me. You have really changed.'

'It's not me that has changed.'

'Since you must know, Emeka has resigned.'

'Precious, is everything OK?' her fiancé called from outside.

'Yes, we're fine, Emeka. We're almost done.'

'If I leave now, Aunty Precious, I won't come back.'

'Then before you go I must tell you a few things. Since you started chasing this revenge—'

'Justice.'

'You want to kill a girl's father because of a letter that was

240

not even addressed to you and you call that justice.'

'Olumide killed my father.'

'And so you will kill hers? The thing Olumide Johnson did to you that was so terrible, you will do it to your friend and say it is justice? I know you. Look at me. You are better than this.'

It would be so easy to let her words draw me into the cowardice dressed as common sense.

'Don't think because I've worked with you for just over a year, you know something about me, Aunty Precious. Mr T, let's go.'

As we walked past her fiancé, I took one last look at his open face. If only he had waited one more day.

Chapter 39

Attractive is not a word that springs to mind when I look at myself in this dress. I should have tried it on but I trusted Tayo and he followed my design. I turned sideways, wondering what else I could wear. No, this was our dress. It was sweet. Women did surgery to make themselves look sweet. I looked over at Cynthia. Not her. If she ever had reconstruction, she'd be aiming for slut.

'We should probably go, Cynthia.'

She continued studying herself.

'Do you think I put enough shimmer on my thighs?'

'Yes.'

'Are you sure?' she asked, her hand hovering dangerously over the tube of sawdust. I moved it out of her reach. If she put on any more, she'd be competing with my fairy lights.

'Yes. I'm sure, Cynthia. Let's go.'

There were already people in the marquee and more were arriving. I had asked the guards to buzz me each time a guest arrived. In the last five minutes, I had lost track of their buzzing. None of them had been my hawker. I couldn't wait any longer.

Cynthia and I walked in silence, or rather I was silent while she worried about her Louboutins getting caked with mud. I had more important things to think about. My hawker and my father were finally going to meet. If I could help it, it would be a very short meeting. I didn't want my hawker getting sucked into a game I was no longer interested in playing.

When we reached the marquee, Cynthia gasped.

'Abikẹ, this is fantastic.'

Nkem had been worth every naira.

After Cynthia had disappeared into the crowd, I walked in, not making eye contact until I was halfway through the tent. Finally someone gathered the courage to speak to me.

'Abikẹ, looking good,' the person said, and the party had officially begun.

I turned to acknowledge the compliment but my reply evaporated. Standing next to Cynthia with his back towards me was a tall boy dressed in an expensive black suit, broad shoulders, tapered torso. It could almost be my father if you added some bulk. Who was he? He turned to face me. I almost didn't recognise him. I let a demure smile play over my lips. That was what I was. Demure in pink for my hawker.

Today I went to Abẹ Bridge and Mr T was gone. He never had much but everything movable had vanished. At this stage both of them were useless. He had helped with the planning, Aunty Precious had brought the money and now the last leg was left for me to run.

The women were still selling the same goods that would

never yield profits large enough for them to escape.

Buy biscuit!

Buy buns!

Buy buttermint!

The same boys were still playing football under the far corner of the bridge. Their talent would never be seen by the scouts from abroad. All this was happening beneath the people who mattered.

When I got home, I filled the five-litre tub with cold water and poured it over my body, until my skin was cool and my mind as clear as glass. I put on the suit that Aunty Precious had paid for. We had bought it from a proper shop, one with attendants who trailed after us, watching Mr T's every move. Even with the clothes I gave him, he still looked out of place.

It is possible that he was once something more than a beggar. While Aunty Precious steered towards the flashier suits with rhinestones on their lapels, Mr T had insisted that the suit be black and quiet.

'We want him to blend in with the millionaires' children so the next day people won't remember him as the boy in the yellow pinstriped suit.'

As I was slipping on the polished black shoes that had also been bought with Aunty Precious's money, I released them. To bear a grudge against anyone that was not Olumide was dangerous. Tonight I needed my full concentration. Aunty Precious and Mr T had done all that they could for me. If at the end, they could not give me their support, their advice and money had been more than enough.

* * *

When I left the room, Jọkẹ was standing by the kitchen sink talking to the Alabi girl.

'Yes, we're leaving in two weeks. My brother found a better job.'

'What do your brother do again?'

'He's a trader.'

'Wow. That's himpressive,' the Alabi girl said, adding a gratuitous aitch.

Today she was wearing jeans that had HOT embroidered on her bottom in red thread.

I cleared my throat.

'Jọkẹ, I'll be back late tonight so don't worry.'

'Who said I would worry?' She smiled as she ran the sponge over a plate. 'You look nice.'

'Yah, very 'andsome.'

'Thank you, Jọkẹ. I hope you've finished packing.'

'Yah.'

My father hated it when we spoke in slang. It was the only time he would ever raise his voice at us.

'I'll see you when I get back. Mummy, I'm going.'

When she came out, she stood by her door, one hand clutching the handle.

'Is it today?'

'Yes, it's my friend's party today.'

She was doing a lot better. She ate meals with us and spoke more often. Yesterday, I'd given Jọkẹ money to take her to the salon, and, with her hair done, she almost looked like her old self.

'Before you go, come and give your mother a hug.'

I let her hold me, feeling the struggle to control her breathing.

'Mummy, why are you hugging him? He's coming back this evening.'

'Come and join us, Jọkẹ,' my mother said. For once, she obeyed without questioning. The three of us stayed linked until Jọkẹ began to fidget. 'This is a touching family moment but I can't stay under your armpit forever.' I let her go and she went back to the dishes.

'Mummy, I'll be late.'

'Go well,' she said, releasing me.

I left the apartment and caught an *okada* to Abby's house. A motorcycle ride was an extravagance but it would be worth a clean entrance. I sat sideways, the dead metal in my pocket resting heavily on my thigh. A hundred metres from her house I stopped the driver, waiting until he had tut-tut-tummed away before walking to her gate. There was no reason for this except natural caution and perhaps a little shame that I would be the only guest arriving by public transport. Better the other guests saw me on foot than on a rusty motorcycle. In the end, I was the only one at the gate when I got there.

'Mr Man, how far?'

'I'm good.'

'You come for party?'

'Yes.'

He brought out a book

'How many time I go tell you, this logbook nah only for people who enter with car. Don't disturb Mr Man again.'

'No, I have to sign. Today I'm just like everybody else.'

Mr T had pointed out that if I were the only guest unaccounted for in the logbook, I would be the chief suspect after tonight.

I wrote my name in capitals and the time flashing on my new watch.

'Enjoy yourself.'

'Thanks.'

As I walked down the driveway, gleaming cars drove past. Some of the guests were hidden by blackened windows, others stared openly at me, the boys challenging, the girls with their caked faces more circumspect. Not one offered a lift. I was glad to walk.

The trees that lined the driveway were roped with fairy lights, their trunks squeezed by these glittering vines. From both sides came the throaty cooing of Olumide's imported doves. For a moment I was tempted to turn and look for the woman in the fountain but I was not sure I could find her on my own. While I was walking, the sky turned from a pink blemished with large spots of orange to a dark, even blue. Again, it was Mr T who pointed out that if the party was held in the evening, I would be certain that Olumide was at home.

From afar, I could feel the air oscillating and by the time I saw the marquee, my whole body was throbbing to the beats blasting from the speakers. It was beautiful, rising into the night like a small hill, its ghostly whiteness offset by the yellow lights strung along its side. An air of expectancy clung to the guests as they walked through the entrance.

I slipped in, scanning the crowd for Abikẹ. Cynthia walked past, momentarily distracting me.

'Hi,' I said.

It was rare to find a good-looking girl like Cynthia flaunt herself till imagination became unnecessary.

'Hello.' She too was looking for someone.

'You look nice.'

'So do you. Are you looking for Abikẹ?'

'Yes. Are you looking for Oritse?'

'Yes,' she said, brushing her hair behind her shoulders to reveal a well-sculpted chest.

'I've seen him.'

I followed her finger and saw Abikẹ standing at the centre of a knot of people, wearing the most hideous dress I have ever seen.

Chapter 40

She is walking towards me and the closer she comes the more awful the dress: shiny pink that sickens in the light, an odd length that turns her normally shapely legs into stumps.

Red silk runs from his neck and ends in a sharp point on the waistband of his trousers. It is a beautiful tie, perhaps worth three weeks of hawking.

I watch Cynthia go and Abby come. The contrast is almost unbearable. Abikẹ refuses to hold my gaze until we—

Hug.
   There is a rough sweaty scent to him that all the layers of clothing cannot hide. I inhale.

Her smell is like the colour of her dress.

I see my mother walking towards us and I turn my hawker towards the food. I don't want him to recognise her. I don't need any unfavourable comparisons tonight.

There's an older woman lurching in our direction whom I assume is Abikẹ's mother. Her face is familiar but I don't know if this is because she was a famous actress or because women with her type of beauty often look alike: hollow cheeks, large eyes, plump lips. Maybe Abby is ashamed of me because she steers us towards the exhaling tureens of food very quickly.

He's not hungry.

I refuse to eat in his house.

All this Chinese food and he says he's not hungry. We separate and I continue to mingle with my guests.
  'Leah. I love that shade of red on you.'

I scan the crowd. There is no sign of Wale, or the Chief or any of Abikẹ's half-siblings. It is to be expected. Oddly, I am disappointed.

'Ikemba, I'm glad you brought your new girlfriend. She wasn't on the guest list but it's always nice to see a new face.'

Three years ago, I knew nothing but a diluted version of this sheltered extravagance. Food that three-quarters of the population would never taste, clothes from places the average Nigerian had never even heard of.

'Tomi, did you buy those shoes in Milan?'

A girl called Leah introduces herself.
　'So what school do you go to?'
　'I dropped out three years ago.'
　She leaves soon after that.

I'm glad to see my hawker mingling. Unfortunately, from the side you can see Leah's dress is too tight for her prominent midriff. Poor girl.

I begin to make my way back to Abby. I have had enough of these children who think make-up and hair extensions equate to worldly knowledge. I bump into Abikẹ's mother.

　'Olu,' she says in a voice teary from alcohol, 'Let's dance like we used to, Olu.'

　'I am not Olu.'

　I take her hand off my suit and she continues moving towards the dance floor, grabbing another young man.

I just saw my mother speaking to my hawker. I hope she didn't say anything ridiculous. I watch as she moves unsteadily to the music, one of the better-looking boys opposite her.

　'No thank you, Oritse. I don't feel like dancing.'

　My father just walked into the tent.

The music is too loud.

'So where is your hawker friend?' my father asks, speaking loudly into my ear.

'You mean you can't spot him? Surely you should be able to tell who doesn't belong.'

He folds his arms. 'Where is he?'

I walk back into the crowd without answering.

'There's someone I want you to meet,' Abby says once I reach her side.

'Who?'

'Just follow me.'

When I see to whom the parting crowd leads, I almost discard the plan. He is a lunge away but I can feel Abikẹ's hand on my arm. I calm myself for this second meeting.

'This is the friend I was telling you about.'

It is a very different Olumide from the one I saw in the corridor. Now he is just another middle-aged father making sure his only daughter is enjoying her party. Of course, he doesn't recognise me.

They shake hands and I am glad to see an equal pressure on both sides.

I return his grip but at the last moment I reduce mine.

'I hear you're a hawker.'

They speak of me.

'I am,' I say.

Most people your age don't have the drive. I'm impressed by your tenacity. That is your ability to work so hard towards achieving your goal.'

The man patronises me.

'I do not entertain strangers in my house lightly but my daughter has vouched for you. Let it remain that way.' They hold eye contact, sizing each other up in that open way only men and wild animals will do.

I drop my gaze first, willing my mind to wander from its proximity to Olumide.

'How much did this tent cost, Abikẹ?' he asks.

When she answers I look at the crowd and blink rapidly.

'And that DJ?'

On and on, until I could write an inventory for this meaningless party.

He is a fool if he thinks this will change things with my hawker. There is indifference on his face when I turn away from my father and though my hawker does not know it, this is our first triumph.

Abbyhawker: 1

Mr Johnson: 0

Soon after, he walks out of the tent, waving to Abikẹ before he disappears into the night. It is time for goodbye.

I make sure my father is gone before I ask, 'Would you like to dance?'

'Pardon?'

'Would you like to dance?' I asked again, taking his hand and turning to the dance floor.

'I have to go,' I said, slipping my hand from her grip. 'I promised Jọkẹ I'd be back early.'

When I knock on his door, I will say, Mr Johnson, it's Abikẹ's friend that hawks. She said I should speak to you privately about work experience.

I take his other hand. 'This is too early. The party just started.'

I have never danced with Abikẹ before. The exposed skin of her back glows. I want to slide my hands along it. There is still time.

He is not leaving for at least another two hours.

She turns her back to me when we reach the dance floor and for a moment I am confused. Has she changed her mind?

I do not want him to see my face.

Then I see the other couples on the dance floor and I understand. My arms fold around her waist, her head leans on my
chest, I press my face into the soft place in her neck and our
feet move.

Just five minutes.

Ten years I could stay like this.

The song ends. 'I should go.'

'No. Let's go somewhere.'

I shake my head but still I ask, 'Where?'
She winks at me. Another first for us.

'The pool.'

We slip into a night that is pockmarked with fairy lights.
There is still time.

Chapter 41

'We can go somewhere else. The fountain is just here.'

'I want some privacy.'

She speaks into my ear, her breath going straight to my head.

He doesn't argue after that but follows with his fingers wrapped around mine.

Sweat holds our hands together.

He doesn't pull away and the moistness begins to grow comfortable.

We are walking through the village garden that Olumide has created on the most expensive real estate in Africa. All over Europe, women have been forced on their backs to pay for these green acres.

I am glad I chose this route because I know how much he loves this place. 'Yeeeeee!'

I whip my hand free. 'What is it?'

I point at the panther, which has moved from the tree to the ground, crouched over a face-down child.

Abby, we've had this.

I take his hand again. 'Let's hurry up.'

She presses herself against me before pulling ahead, dragging me behind her, and before I know it we've reached the house.

Then the front hall.

Then the staircase.

Then the corridor.

Then we are here and I do not know what to expect.

Chapter 42

As we enter the glass room with the pool, I reach for the zip on her dress. The outside lights shimmer on the water, the air hums from the faraway music and my fingers find themselves on the iron tracks that run down her back. She pulls away and her zip scratches my index finger.

Do you think we are strange?

'What?' I reach for her arm but grasp air.

Five steps get me to the pool ledge, the points of my shoes poking over safety.
    'I said, do you think we are strange?'

'What do you mean?'
    She turns sideways and lets one shoe skim water.

'You are a hawker, I am a Johnson. Did you never find that strange?'

'Explain.'

'Just answer me.'

The impatience in her tone is irritating. 'Yes, of course I found it strange.'

Me too.

'And since we are asking questions, let me ask mine. Why me?'

'What do you mean?'

'Just answer.'

His voice is harsh and the words abrupt, barely spoken before he cuts them off.

She ignores me, slipping off her right shoe and then her left, pulling her dress down until it stops at her knees. I check my watch. There is no time.

'Tell me why you chose me.'

I say the words before I realise they are stained with gratitude.

'Because you ran.'

'Pardon?' I ask, unable to catch her mumbling.

I said I chose you because you ran, and because you were hand-some and you didn't speak like a hawker.

She shouts, taking off her bracelet and flinging it on the blue tiles.

 'You mean—'

No, I did not want your ice cream.

'And—'

Yes, it was a test.

'Your car breaking down.'

Was not real.

She'd planned everything. Oritse's singing, Cynthia, the money on the road, visits to her house. 'What kind of person are you?' She turns her head.

When I see his expression, I face the pool again. 'I don't know.'

I stretch out to touch her but her arms are folded and her shoulders raised. She doesn't look like she wants to be touched.

 'Abikẹ, I have to go.'

She shrugs.

'OK, Mister Mysterious.'

'What do you mean?' I ask, as I move closer to hug her.

'Why don't you just come out and tell me that you were rich before your father died?'

I stop. 'What do you know about my father's death?' She shrugs again.

'Nothing more than you've told me.'

'Who told you I was rich?'

'Don't be ridiculous. You told me yourself.'

I'd never mentioned that we were rich. I'd told her about the car accident but I had never mentioned money. What else did she know? 'Abịkẹ, what do you know about my father's death?'

'He died early, his death made you poor, it was sudden.'

'What did you say?'

His tone grates.

I watch as she deliberately takes off her second shoe, then her left earring, the right, and the clips that fasten her hair.

'What do you think you're doing?'

I ignore him.

She bends her elbows to reach her zip but her fingers come short.

'Help me.'

'What do you know about my father?' Is that why she came to the road? Had she been sent?

My fingers finally brush the tip of the zip and I feel him watching.

She slides her dress open to reveal skin I had wanted to touch.

I am standing in my underwear now, still he has not taken another step towards me.

She crouches on the ledge, about to fall into the pool when—

He takes my arm.

'Abikẹ, tell me what you know about my father.'

'How many times have I told you?'

'When have I ever—'

'My name is Abby.'

It is the most natural thing. My hands find their way to her neck and once they are there, they stay there.

'How dare you t—'

My grip tightens. Her hands pummel my face, catching the corner of my eye, forcing tears from my cornea.

The disadvantage is mine. He is standing and I am crouched.

Her nails claw me and blood begins to dribble from my left cheek.

Why?

She spits, a weak spurt that runs down her chin and on to my hands.

This is what happens when you trust a hawker.

Mr T was right.

I should have listened to my father.

To kill the plant you kill the seed.

I should have been more like him.

Tears are falling on to my hands now and they sting where she has scratched me.

I should have known.

Mucus joins the tears, a lubricant between my palms and her neck.

He will pay.

She is almost gone. I can feel the pulsing in her neck growing weaker. Suddenly, the thought of holding her dead in my hands repulses me. Let the water finish it if it can. I am going to kill Olumide.

I do not realise I am released until I splash into the pool.

Turning I hear the click of a switch.

The room floods with light.

Chapter 43

'*What is going on here?*'

I watch as Abikẹ pulls herself out of the pool. Her elbows are weak, she falters but when I offer her a hand, she spits.

'*Abikẹ, what is this?*'

She is standing next to me now, her cotton underwear sagging from the dripping water.

'*What are you doing with this boy from the gutter? In my house—*' *He stops, squinting as he takes a step towards us.* '*Are those marks on your neck?*'

I do not want her to see but there is no time to lead him off to his parlour and put the bullet in his head. He might scream for help on the way. He might attack me. 'Olumide,' I say, placing my trembling hand on my pocket, feeling the reassuring weight, 'does the name Sodipo mean anything to you?'

That is all? That is all he came to say? His surname registers nothing. My father does not even glance at him. 'This boy put those marks on you.'

I cannot see the marks but I can feel where my hawker's fingers were pressed into my neck only a few moments ago.

'Olumide,' I say again, my eyes avoiding the imprints my fingers have made. There is no time for guilt.

'Abikẹ, how could you be so foolish? One of my rivals has tried to get to me through you!'

'Olumide!' I shout, my fingers patting my pocket again. 'Stop your lies and answer me.'

There is something inside there. My father has seen it too, though his eyes have neither left the hawker's face nor strayed to mine.

'After everything I've taught you,' he continues in a tone that becomes increasingly agitated. 'You couldn't see it? You were blinded by a handsome face. Abikẹ!'

'He's lying,' I say, trying to catch her eye but she does not look at me.

For the first time my father and I are playing together, trying to distract this boy into revealing what he has in his pocket.

'You're right. I should have known.'

Despite myself, I feel betrayed when she agrees with Olumide.

'Of course you should have known,' my father says, looking at me and taking a step towards the hawker. 'Think about it, Abikẹ.'

I don't know if what he is saying is true but I must play now and think later.

'Yes,' I say, raising my hand to my mouth.

I cannot let myself be distracted. Once she has watched me shoot her father, she can never remember me fondly.

'What other reason could there be?' my father asks, staring at the hawker and drawing his attention from me.

Somehow, the distance between myself and Olumide has lessened and if I don't act now, it will be too late. I lower my hand.

Before his fingers can close on anything, I slide my hand into his pocket, grasp the thing and pull it out. It is so easy that I laugh when I see the gun dangling from my grip.

I lunge at her,

When I toss the gun into the water, it makes a splashing noise before sinking to the bottom.

'Abikẹ!'

They both say my name and I can tell from my father's voice that he did not wish to prolong the issue.

I look at the gun, its shape undistorted by the clear water and for a moment, panic threatens to overwhelm me. Then I remember Mr T's Plan C for if I did not kill Olumide and he did not kill me.

'You must not go home,' he had said. 'It is the first place they will look for you since the girl knows your house. You must find another Abẹ Bridge and disappear into Lagos for a few weeks, maybe even months.' My mother and Jọkẹ may think but the worst but it would not be forever.

How had Abikẹ, the grandmaster of Frustration, missed that the boy I called my hawker did not exist? My pride is the thing most bruised.

The distance between myself and the open door will take less than a second to cover. They do not call me Runner G for nothing.

'Why did you do it?'

Her voice, toneless and painful, stops me.

'There's no need to ask such a question,' my father says, taking

another step towards the hawker. 'I've told you. One of my rivals sent him.'

Even now that I know I will never see her again, a part of me still cares for her opinion. There is still time.

'Abikẹ, your father murdered mine.'

I give him the benefit of the doubt and this is all he can come up with?

'Who was your father?'

I know my father. He is capable of murder but not for everyone.

She does not believe me but still, she is asking questions. 'Look, I have proof that he murdered my father and proof for other things as well. Do you remember the woman I worked with, Aunty Precious. She was sold into prostitution by your father. He's a murderer and a pimp. I have proof. Signed letters, witnesses, documents.' But she is not listening, or rather she is listening but she is not hearing.

'You tried to kill me because my father killed your father.'

'You don't understand. You asked me to come here, you led me on, you confused me.'

That first day on the road returned to me. I had been sitting in the back seat, we had caught eyes and without my beckoning, he had walked towards me already aware of who I was. I re-

membered his suggestions. Have the party outside, make sure your parents are there, keep the noise and the people who might stumble on us sealed in a canopy.

'Who sent you?'

Had she heard anything I'd been saying? One last time, I would explain. 'It wasn't about you. My father—'

'It wasn't about me?' I shriek, despite my effort to keep my voice calm.

'No it wasn't.' Not when I came to your house this evening. Why did you have to mention my father? Why couldn't you just have said goodbye?

'You tried to reach my father by killing me and it wasn't about me?'

I will always be the quickest route to Olumide Johnson for the Michaels and hawkers of this world. Looking for something to hold, I see my stiletto lying by the pool. With the full upward thrust of my hand, I smash its heel into the side of his face.

I react without thinking.

My father moves fast.

Before I can wrest the shoe from her grip—

The hawker's arms are pinned behind his back.

I struggle but he is stronger. I kick but he forces me down till my knees are touching the ground.

'Abikẹ, it seems you want to play with your food.' He twists his head until he can see his watch. 'Hurry up. I have things to do.'

She grips the arch of the shoe and looks straight into my eyes. There is no Abikẹ in that gaze. Only her second self, Abby.

You slithered into my confidence.

'Your father killed mine,' I say. 'He is a pimp, he has killed others, he—' The heel lands in my mouth and drags along my gums.

You deceived me.

The stiletto slits down the front of my shirt, scattering buttons and exposing my chest.

I threw a party for you.

Systematically, she lands wherever my skin is torn from our first struggle. I cannot plead with my eyes, they are swelling.

I changed my name for you.

Once, she winces after a blow to the temple that makes me scream but the shoe and her left hand never stop moving.

You deserve whatever happens next.

Through a narrowing slit, I see the blood on my shirt.

Abruptly my father shoves the hawker forward and his face thuds into the ground. 'Enough. You have learnt your lesson.'
    I wipe sweat from my cheeks.
    'What should I do with him?'

I try to rise but Olumide presses his foot on my neck.

Looking at the blood dripping on to the white tiles, then the mouth that it is coming from, I do not know what I want my father to do to the hawker.

As the pressure from Olumide's foot pushes me into unconsciousness, I remember Jọkẹ and my mother and how I left them in the flat. They will wait one day, then two, then a year, then a decade, never knowing what happened to me.

'Release him.'

My eyes flutter painfully open. 'What?'
    My hands push against the floor but his shoe moves to my neck, grinding me into the tiles.

'I said release him.'

Hope begins to rise through me. Perhaps I will see them to-night.

'Abikẹ, don't be silly.'

I lie still.

'It's bad enough that you let him deceive you. To reward him and the people that sent him by letting him go?'

Still she does not answer.

'Abikẹ?'

A second, lighter foot joins his.

'The people that sent him think killing him is the worst you can do.'

He laughs, a deep, uncontrolled laughter of a man who is very amused.

'What do you intend?'

I strain to hear what Abby will say.

While I am thinking, my father kneels, the full weight of his body pressing down on the hawker's back. Slowly, he bends until his mouth is hovering over his ear like an insect over a flower.

'Emmanuel Toyosi Sodipo,' Olumide whispers. 'You look just like him.'

Whatever my father says, the effect is immediate. The hawker's back arches, his legs struggle but he is pinned down.
    'What did you say?'
    'I just told him something he needed to hear.'
    'What?'
    My resolve falters.
    'What did he say to you?' *I say prodding the hawker with my foot.*

I lift my head, struggling to speak but Olumide kicks me down and my teeth bang against the slick, metallic tiles.

'Abikẹ, I don't—'
    'One of you answer me!'

'He killed my father,' I finally manage, my lips pushing against the floor and slurring the words.

'What? Let him speak.'

The pressure on my head is reduced. 'He killed my father,' I splutter, 'and he just said his name. That was what he said

274

just now.' The effort leaves me coughing blood on to the floor.

'Is this true?'

One ear is pressed to the ground and I hear Olumide walking away before I feel that he is no longer on top of me. I twist my head to see him standing in front of Abikẹ, his body almost completely blocking her.

I look up and his eyes are hard. 'Abikẹ, I'm only going to tell you once. This boy was sent by a rival.'

When had he become so sure? A few minutes ago it had only been a possibility. 'What did you say to him just now?'

When he answers his words are slow and sharp and clear. 'You either believe me or you believe this boy.'

I see the figure before they do but I cannot tell who it is, blood hazes my vision.

I see him but I do not know who he is. 'Oh, it's you,' my father says.

Who is it?

'Get out and forget what you've seen tonight,' he paused before adding, 'for your own good.'

'I should forget?' a male voice says in a rasping tone I have heard before.

The stranger steps forward and I recognise him.

'Did you think we wouldn't find out?'

'Get out of this place,' my father says, turning from my half-brothers and walking towards the hawker.

'We heard about your new will,' the voice says, closer now.

My father stops. 'And so what?

'You can't cut us out like that.'

'And who is to stop me?'

'Me.'

When the bullet enters my father, he stands up straighter, his shoulders broad and menacing and for a moment it seems he is invincible. The boy shrinks. I wait for my father to deal with him but nothing happens. His raised arm hangs in the air and then he topples into the pool, a thick ribbon of blood swirling from his chest.

The boom of a gun resounds, a heavy object falls, plummets, crashes past my ear and smacks into water.

I want to scream but there is no time for screaming. The empty hole of the gun is staring at my face.

'Give me a reason not to shoot,' the voice says. It is male.

'I've read the will. If I die, next in line are two charities and his old university.'

'You're lying.'

'Kill me then but just know you'll be doing it for charity.'
    He smiles when I say this and I see his teeth are like mine, small with his gums drooping lower than normal.

'Who is that?' I hear him say.

He points at the hawker.
    'Someone I used to know,' I say, gathering my clothes, unembarrassed by his stares.

'Is he the one that did that to you?'

He points at my neck.
    'Go and see what I did to him,' I say, slipping my dress over my head.

I feel someone standing over me but when I try to look up, his face is covered in moving lights.

'Why are you looking at him like that? Do you know him?' I ask the boy who is still staring down at the hawker now that I am dressed and ready to go.

'He looks like a friend of mine.'

I see the hawker's gun still lying at the bottom of the pool where I flung it. 'Please get that.'

'And if I don't?'

'Then shoot me. I am too tired.'

There is another splash.

He comes out of the pool holding the gun.
    'Take off your clothes and wring them,' I say, 'or else a trail of water will follow us.'
    He strips to a tattered pair of underwear. Now he is the one that looks ridiculous. I scan the room one last time.
    'Let us go and discuss. We'll go to my living room,' I say curtly. The tone of our relationship must be set now.

As I slip into unconsciousness it becomes so obvious who the second person is, that the realisation almost pushes me back into consciousness. Almost.

We leave the pool room with his weight between us. When I switch off the light, my father is left floating in the darkness

278

and for a moment I falter but it is only a moment. He would want it this way.

Epilogue

ABIKẸ

'Speak to Dosunmu,' I say for the fifth time today. I worry that I am growing too dependent on him but Dosunmu is the only one who knows anything about the companies and loyalties and factions I have acquired by being my father's sole heir.

They would not take me seriously at first. I am an eighteen-year-old woman who has chosen to run Johnson Corporations instead of going to university. They did not know that for seven years I had learnt more from playing Frustration than any of them had ever learnt in a textbook.

I studied the picture that had arrived from Dubai. Hassan was rounder now; a small mound was beginning to rise under his shirt and he was smiling with one arm slung round the neck of a camel. He had been superb in the witness box. In monosyllabic answers, he denied everything the prosecution levelled at him but refused to explain how his fingerprints had gotten on the gun, what the gun was doing in his room, why his diary was filled with pages detailing his hatred of his oga.

'Aunty. Shop is doing well,' I read off the back before running the photo through a shredder.

It would not do for the wrong person to see this picture of a man supposedly dead by firing squad. Newly promoted Commissioner Julius might want a second bribe for sneaking Hassan out of jail the night before he was meant to be shot. I would have to make sure Hassan stopped sending these.

At first, I considered letting Wale reap the consequences of his actions. I thought of the scandal. Johnson fratricide. Johnson kills Johnson. Father vs Son. So in exchange for him persuading his brothers to give up their claims to my inheritance, I allowed him to walk free. I did not leave them penniless but it is clear that what they have is from my magnanimity. To think the fool believed my father would leave his billions to charity.

I considered making the hawker take the fall. One testimony from me would have damned him but again – the scandal. No doubt he would have brought up the issue of my father having killed his. Perhaps other allegations would have been raised and they might have stuck. Johnson killer. Killer Johnson. Pimp Johnson.

Suggesting Hassan was genius. Not that everything Dosunmu suggests is genius. He thought we should have found the hawker and at least threatened his family. I was not interested. The more I thought of that night, the more I was unsure who to believe. Was he sent? Did my father murder his? Dosunmu thought my questions irrelevant. Either way the hawker knew too much but were he to speak, he would have implicated him-

self. To save his family, he would remain silent and lose his integrity. It was a gamble but almost a year has passed and my way has proved right.

Dosunmu will find in the coming years that I am not my father, though the more I understand the webs my father wove, the more I respect the man. Sometimes, I wish he were the one explaining the rudiments of a rigging to me instead of his stooge, who after years of double dealings cannot speak in plain English.

Sometimes I think I even miss him. It should have been him standing behind me when I saw my first supplicant. If he had been there, this Bank MD would not have had the temerity to glance past me and ask, 'Dosunmu, what is going on here?' Yet, despite this posthumous esteem, I am not my father. There are industries formerly affiliated to Johnson Corporations that I have severed all contact with. As I have explained to my inherited stooge, they tarnish my brand.

That the hawker was right about the trafficking does not mean my father is guilty of murder. There is no record of it, not that he would have been stupid enough to leave one, but Dosunmu denies it.

'It was fortuitous that Sodipo died in that accident. It put an end to the case he was building.' That was all he would say. When I pressed he replied, 'Abikẹ, don't waste your time on the past. We have more serious issues on our hands now.'

I noted the 'we' but I let his slip pass. He was right. I had more serious things to worry about. Some of my father's companies were trying to force me out of my position as CEO. There was no time for wondering who killed the hawker's father. Even

if he had been telling the truth, what then? Would I drop
everything to go back to a boy that had almost strangled me to
death?

'*Dosunmu, have you spoken to the Vice Chancellor of*
UNILAG about my plans for an Olumide Johnson Recreation
Centre?'

'*Yes, ma.*'

'*Also, Dosunmu, next month I want you to stay in the Delta*
and see what's happening on my rigs.'

'*Yes, ma.*'

I picked up the phone and dialled the reception.

'*Send in the Minister.*'

THE HAWKER

I leave the flat and turn on to the road. Tonight my street has
light and everyone is taking advantage of the electricity. I am
invited to play snooker. I decline. I am invited to dinner. I
decline. I see two men facing each other in the street. I move
closer. They are about to fight. I am not in the mood. There
is nothing to do in my area. I return home and go to sleep.

The next afternoon I wake not knowing what to do. It is
Sunday. I do not hawk on Sundays. The money I make is too
little to hand over 90 per cent.

'So you are finally awake.'

'Yes.'

She tells me about her mock exams. She did well. She
is on track for engineering. All my savings are for her uni-

versity. I have heard enough for now. She keeps talking.

'My teacher thinks that five of us will—'

'Jọkẹ, please not now.'

It is always like this when I am home. They clamour for my attention because they do not know how worthless I am.

'Where are you going?'

I turn on to the road walking restlessly. She is everywhere: polished into the black jeep that glides by, reflected in the pupils of a young hawker, ground into the dust of the road. It is Sunday. No one is fighting. I want to run until she is driven from my head.

There was nothing I could do. Had I spoken, it would have been my word against hers. She helped her father's killer escape; she killed an innocent man in the killer's place. What could I have done against such forces? You could have spoken. You could have shown yourself your father's son instead of a bastard coward that even now, is relieved to be alive.

When I get back to our block, the boys have come out for their evening smoke.

'Boyo, how far?'

'Rambo I dey. How body?'

'It cool. You wan smoke?'

'Not tonight.'

I walk into the apartment and see Jọkẹ and my mother talking by the sink.

'Hello. Are you hungry? Mummy and I made Mile 12 pottage.'

We came back to Mile 12 for the trial. We had spent three weeks in Ogun State when my mother brought me a newspaper with the headline: DRIVER ARRESTED FOR JOHNSON MURDER.

'I borrowed it from our neighbour when I saw the headline. Is this you?'

'I didn't do anything, Mummy. Stop whispering.'

'It happened the night you came back with your face bruised, didn't it? You looked like someone returning from a serious battle. Did he put up—'

'Mummy, I didn't do anything.'

'I know you didn't and if anybody asks that is what I will say, but this man,' she said, pointing at the picture of Hassam, 'did he do it too? If two adults plan something and only one escapes, it is nobody's fault.'

'I don't know what—'

'I've heard. You don't know anything but you did well. You've given your mother peace of mind and brought justice for many people.'

I had to go back. Since I was to take part in the trial, I could not leave my mother and Jọkẹ in a strange city, in a flat that was rented for three months. When we got to Mile 12, the landlord had tenants ready to move in. We had paid five years' rent and lived there only three. After shouting and waving of contracts, he gave us back the keys to our flat. It was then the doubts came.

What if nobody believed me? I would have thrown away everything for nothing. I would come under suspicion. What use would I be to Hassan then? I stayed silent, following the trial, promising I would step in at the next development, and the next, until the man was dead and I was as guilty as she and her half-brother. I am a disgrace to my father.

'Diogu m,' my mother says to me. 'Diogu m, we made yam pottage for you. Please come and eat.'

This has become her name for me since she read those headlines.

'Mummy, please don't call me that. I am not a warrior.'

'Diogu m, you are my warrior.'

I wish I could tell her what really happened that night. I fear the news her *diogu* is a spineless coward would force her into a relapse. She is better now. She teaches at the nursery school, she talks to her daughter, and I will not rob her of this.

'Mummy, thank you. Let me just wash my hands and I'll come and join you.'

Acknowledgements

It takes a whole village to write a book so I'd like to acknowledge some of the villagers who helped along the way. Many thanks go to:

My father, Dr Okey Onuzo for all his support, teaching and prayer.

My mother, Dr Mariam Onuzo for always sharing in my triumphs and failures.

My sisters Dilichi Lawal for investing in my writing and Dinachi Onuzo for her encouragement.

My brothers Chinaza Onuzo and Kassim Lawal who read the early drafts.

My extended siblings Chidinma Chigbo, Ngozi Okerulu, Ifeanyi Okoye, Funlola Ekundayo and Olusegun Ekundayo who stayed up one night and plotted the first draft with me.

My cousins Ebube Onuzo, Opeyemi Atawo and Chidinma Onuzo for their insightful criticisms.

Aunty Sola Adegbomire for helping me with legal research.

My friends Melanie Cheng, Claudia Li, Moyo Kupoluyi, Sharon Lo and Olivia Digby who commented honestly.

My teachers Ms Jackie Askew, Mrs Nicola Young and Ms Janet Thomas, who taught me to write carefully and concisely.

Reverend Terry Hemming.

My earlier English teachers, Mrs Dafeta, Mrs Andieke, Mrs Onafowakan.

Pastor Bajo Akisanya for his prayers and advice.

Aunty Angela, Aunty Vero and Aunty Hope who changed my diapers.

Many thanks to Rosie Apponyi for rescuing me from the slush pile, Georgina Capel my lovely agent and of course Sarah Savitt, my editor, for the countless hours given to making this book better.